10/68

Newford

DINGO

FIREBIRD
WHERE FANTASY TAKES FLIGHT™

BOOKS BY CHARLES DE LINT

The Riddle of the Wren
Moonheart: A Romance
The Harp of the Grey Rose
Mulenegro: A Romany Tale
Yarrow: An Autumn Tale
Jack, the Giant Killer
Greenmantle
Wolf Moon
Svaha
The Valley of Thunder
Drink Down the Moon
Ghostwood
Angel of Darkness
(as Samuel M. Key)
The Dreaming Place
The Little Country
From a Whisper to a Scream
(as Samuel M. Key)
Spiritwalk
Dreams Underfoot (collection)
Into the Green
I'll Be Watching You
(as Samuel M. Key)
The Wild Wood
Memory and Dream
The Ivory and the Horn (collection)
Jack of Kinrowan
Trader

Someplace to Be Flying
Moonlight and Vines (collection)
Forests of the Heart
Triskell Tales: 22 Years of Chapbooks
(collection)
The Road to Lisdoonvarna
The Onion Girl
Seven Wild Sisters
(illustrated by Charles Vess)
A Handful of Coppers (collection)
Waifs and Strays (collection)
Tapping the Dream Tree (collection)
A Circle of Cats
(illustrated by Charles Vess)
Spirits in the Wires
Medicine Road
(illustrated by Charles Vess)
The Blue Girl
Quicksilver and Shadow (collection)
The Hour Before Dawn (collection)
Triskell Tales 2 (collection)
Widdershins
Promises to Keep
Little (Grrl) Lost
Dingo

DINGO

Charles de Lint

FIREBIRD

AN IMPRINT OF PENGUIN GROUP (USA) INC.

FIREBIRD

Published by the Penguin Group

Penguin Group (USA) Inc., 345 Hudson Street, New York, New York 10014, U.S.A.

Penguin Group (Canada), 90 Eglinton Avenue East, Suite 700, Toronto, Ontario, Canada M4P 2Y3
(a division of Pearson Penguin Canada Inc.)

Penguin Books Ltd, 80 Strand, London WC2R 0RL, England

Penguin Ireland, 25 St Stephen's Green, Dublin 2, Ireland
(a division of Penguin Books Ltd)

Penguin Group (Australia), 250 Camberwell Road, Camberwell, Victoria 3124, Australia
(a division of Pearson Australia Group Pty Ltd)

Penguin Books India Pvt Ltd, 11 Community Centre, Panchsheel Park,
New Delhi - 110 017, India

Penguin Group (NZ), 67 Apollo Drive, Rosedale, North Shore 0632,
New Zealand (a division of Pearson New Zealand Ltd.)

Penguin Books (South Africa) (Pty) Ltd, 24 Sturdee Avenue,
Rosebank, Johannesburg 2196, South Africa

Registered Offices: Penguin Books Ltd, 80 Strand, London WC2R 0RL, England

First published by Firebird, an imprint of Penguin Group (USA) Inc., 2008

1 3 5 7 9 10 8 6 4 2

LIBRARY OF CONGRESS CATALOGING-IN-PUBLICATION DATA
De Lint, Charles, 1951-
Dingo / a novella by Charles de Lint.
p. cm. Summary: Seventeen-year-old Miguel Schreiber and a long-term enemy are drawn into a
strange dream world when they fall in love with shapeshifting sisters from Australia--twins hiding
from a cursed ancestor who can only be freed with the girls' cooperation.

[1. Supernatural--Fiction. 2. Space and time--Fiction. 3. Sisters--Fiction. 4. Twins--Fiction.
5. Dingo--Fiction. 6. Fathers and sons--Fiction. 7. Single-parent families--Fiction. 8. Mythology,
Aboriginal Australian--Fiction.] I. Title.
PZ7.D383857Din 2008
[Fic]--dc22
2007031716

ISBN 978-0-14-240816-2

Printed in the United States of America

for my
Aussie muso pals
Paul and Julie,
here's to our
next road trip

for their daughter
Charlotte Molly

and for the dingo girls.
Jenna and Caitlin

No one likes to think it of their father, but there are days when I can't help but feel that somehow I got stuck with the biggest loser of all loser dads. It's mostly on days like this when he's off on a house call to buy new stock and I'm stuck minding the store.

MIKE'S USED COMICS & RECORDS, the sign says above the door in paint that's chipped and starting to fade.

Okay, so he's not a deadbeat, because ever since Mom died, he's always made sure we have food on the table and a roof over our heads. And some kids might think it was cool to have a dad so into comics and music. But try living with it, day in and day out. It's Superman this, and Spider-Man that, and wow, a Grateful Dead boot with a version of some song that they only ever played live one or two times and never recorded officially.

"Who cares?" is not something Dad hears when he's ramped up about some hot new find.

And then there's my hand-me-down clothes. T-shirts with logos of bands I've never heard of—or if I have, I usually don't like. Jeans and cords that forced me to learn how to sew so that I could take them in and not look like a complete geek. At least I get my own shoes—I'm a size nine and he's an eleven—and socks and underwear.

I guess I'm making it sound worse than it is. It's not *all* hand-me-downs. When we're flush, I get new clothes. The trouble is, too often the money that comes in goes out to cover general expenses and new stock, and there's nothing much left over for luxuries like a new winter jacket.

But you know, there are kids who don't even have one parent who loves them as much as Dad does me, so I'm not really complaining. I just hate getting stuck in the store, where I have to pretend to have as much enthusiasm as I do the knowledge I've picked up by osmosis.

And there are benefits.

The issue of *Classics Illustrated* that I need for a book report is always there, and since Dad finally caved and started handling CDs as well as vinyl and cassettes a couple of years ago, I get my pick of current music. We have this one DJ who trades new releases for old vinyl, and she's often got stuff that won't even be available in a regular store for a couple of months. When I get tired of the disc, I just stick it back in the sales bin.

And then there are the girls.

At school, they don't even look twice at me, but here in the store, the music junkies strike up conversations and hang out, listening to the classic rock music we've got playing in the store. I can put up with hours of the Kinks or Hendrix if I have a pretty girl to talk to while those old albums are playing.

Today I'm not expecting much. It's almost closing time, school's been out for a couple of hours, and everybody's already gone home or to the mall. Downtown, Harnett's Point isn't exactly hopping in late April. It won't get busy until the *turistas* show up for the summer.

The shop is longer than it's wide, with a counter just this side of the front door, and then bins running down to the back along either wall, with display racks above them, except at the back, where the newest CDs are displayed in a tall wire floor rack. Cases only, of course. We keep the actual disc behind the counter. Beside the CD rack is the door that leads to the basement, the toilet, and the claustrophobic storage area in the rear of the store.

Classic posters hang above the racks, laminated and mounted, most of them signed. The Stones. Chuck Berry. Bonnie Raitt. Phil Ochs. Bruce Springsteen.

The floor's tiled, which makes it easy to mop up in the winter—my job—and to sweep in the summer—also my job. But right now the floor's clean, everything's been dusted and remerchandised, and I'm ensconced behind the counter on a tall stool, a copy of today's newspaper open in front of me. The remains of a takeout coffee from Rudi's down the street is growing cold by the register. On the sound system I've got a boot of a Joe Strummer concert with great versions of some Jimmy Cliff and Ramones covers.

Okay, maybe I gave the wrong impression. It's not that I don't like music. It's not even that I don't like obscure music, or bootlegs. It's just that I don't obsess over it like Dad. For me, it's all about how it sounds. For him, half the thrill is the pedigree of the pressing, or some arcane bit of trivia attached to the recording session.

So I listen to the Arctic Monkeys and Broken Social Scene, and whatever else is currently cool, but I like the classics, too. My classics just don't go as far back as Dad's and don't involve a story to go with the production credits.

Anyway, I'm flipping through the newspaper, watching the minute hand inch toward closing time, and checking out the odd passerby on the street—I'm great at multitasking—when I see her.

Ever have one of those moments when everything just

kind of stops and it feels as though the whole universe is focused on this one thing that's got your attention?

That's what it's like when I see her go by the window, hesitate at the door to look behind her, and then come in. It's gray and dismal outside, but she's got the sun in her hair—long, red-gold tangles that are frizzing because of the damp and give her a halo. And here's a funny thing: she's got a large dog at her side with fur the exact same color as her hair. The dog's about the size of a large German shepherd—similar body shape, but the chest isn't as deep, and the hips are slimmer. It looks more like one of those mutts you might see up on the rez. The fur's short like a rez dog's. The under chin and belly are white, but the rest of its coat really is the exact same color as the girl's hair.

And they both have the same brown eyes.

She's got a slender, boyish figure, but that's the only boy-ish thing about her. There's a spray of freckles on her nose and under her eyes. Her skin is the warm brown of a late summer tan, which I didn't think was usual for a redhead.

"Hi," she says.

I realize I've been staring at her. I bob my head and smile. "Hi, yourself," I say.

"Can I bring my dog in?"

"Is he house-trained?"

"She's a she, and yes."

"Then, sure."

Dad wouldn't like it, but Dad's not here.

"I love your accent," I say. "Where are you from?"

"Australia."

"Wow, that's a long way."

She nods. "And I like your accent, too," she adds.

"I don't have an accent."

She smiles. "You do to me."

"I guess I do."

Through the window behind her, I see Johnny Ward on the sidewalk across the street, flanked by the Miller brothers, Nick and Brandon. They're standing there looking at the store, and I get the feeling that they're the reason the girl's come inside, though why she should be worried about a few bullies with that big dog at her side, I don't know. Sure, Ward and the Millers are brawny and formidable, but her dog doesn't exactly look like a pushover.

"Were those guys bothering you?" I ask.

She shrugs. "Not really. They're just creepy, and the guy in the middle's been sort of following me."

"Well, don't worry. They won't come in here."

"Why not?"

I smile. "Do you want the long answer or the short one?"

She looks over her shoulder, across the street. "The long one. That means I can stay here longer."

God, I love this accent. It makes the simplest sentences sound exotic.

"You can stay as long as you want," I assure her, "whether someone's following you or not."

She cocks her head. "You're nice."

I have a dark cast to my complexion, but that doesn't mean a blush won't show. I duck my head.

"Yeah, well . . ." I point to the spare stool behind the counter. "Have a seat, and I'll tell you the story of Johnny Ward's one and only humiliation—or at least it's the only one I know of."

"My name's Lainey," she says as she hoists herself up.

The dog lies down on the floor beside the stool and rests her head on her paws.

"I'm Miguel," I tell her. "What's Lainey short for?"

"Nothing. It's just my name." She grins and sticks out her hand. "Pleased to meet you."

She even has freckles on the back of her hand, I see as we shake.

"So why won't those boys come in here?" she asks.

"Oh, the Miller brothers could if they wanted, but not Johnny. His family—the Wards—have lived here forever, and they all walk around with a chip on their shoulder.

Their lives have always been a mess, but of course it's never their fault.

"Anyway, Johnny came swaggering in here one Saturday afternoon last year, acting like he owned the place. No surprise there, but he started hassling a couple of kids, back there in the CD section. Then he pushed one of them against the floor rack and the whole thing came down, so Dad went back and asked him to leave.

"I have to tell you this about my dad. He's really easy-going—the kind of guy everybody likes—but you just don't want to push him too hard.

"Johnny didn't know, or he didn't care. He just looked at Dad and said, 'I suppose you're going to make me.'

"Well, Dad didn't say anything for a long moment. I guess Johnny thought it was because he was scared, but I knew better. Dad was just trying to keep his temper in check.

" 'What do you say, old man?' Johnny said, really pushing his luck now. 'Think you've got the cojones?'

" 'Here's the thing,' Dad finally said. 'You're going to walk out that door by yourself, or I'm going to take you out. And if I take you out, I'm going to beat the crap out of you. Now, you might think if I do that, you'll press charges against me, but you know what? I'll be happy to do a few months in county just to have the satisfaction of wiping that smirk from your face.'

" 'You can't—' Johnny began, but Dad cut him off.

" 'Oh, and I know what you're thinking,' he said. 'You can walk out right now and go running to the cops to press charges against me for uttering threats. Or maybe send your old man, or one of your loser uncles, to teach me a lesson. Well, the same deal holds, kid. I'll recover, do my time in county—if it comes to that—but when I get out, I'll still beat the crap out of you.'

" 'You're psycho,' Johnny said.

"Dad nodded. 'Now you're getting it. And here's something else I want you to remember. You might be thinking of coming back, maybe throw a rock through the window, maybe set a little fire out back. But I'm telling you here and now, anything ever happens to this place—I don't care if you did it or not—I'll beat the crap out of you again. Are you starting to see a pattern yet?' "

As I'm telling the story, I suddenly realize how redneck and mean this all sounds. Way to impress the new girl, I think, but by the time the realization hits me, I've gone too far not to finish up. So I take it to the end as quickly as I can, with Johnny beating a hasty retreat.

"He slunk out of here," I say, "and he hasn't been back.

He doesn't even bug me at school anymore—and he sure used to."

"And he never tried to do anything later?" Lainey asks.

I shake my head. "No. He'll even cross the street rather than walk on the sidewalk in front of the store."

"What about his family? Did, like, his dad come and give yours a hard time or anything?"

"No. Look," I add, "I know how this story sounds, and I guess I just wasn't thinking. It's not the kind of story I usually tell about my dad. Mostly I just goof on him for being so into comic books and weird records."

"It's okay."

"No, it's not. That story makes my dad seem like a bad guy, and he's not. He just doesn't like bullies."

"So who does?" Lainey says. "And he doesn't sound like a bad guy. He sounds tough. Where I come from, that's not such a bad thing." She looks around the store, taking in the comics in their Mylar bags, the signed posters on the wall. "But how come your dad *is* so tough?"

I smile. "He didn't always have a store like this. He used to be a biker. He always says that if it wasn't for Mom, he'd be dead or in jail right now. She's the one who turned him around, made him, quote, a better man than he could ever have hoped to be if he'd never met her."

"I guess mothers can do that," she says, "if the dad even bothers to stick around."

"Your dad ran out on your family?"

She shrugs. "He was never there long enough except to get Mum pregnant."

"That sucks."

"But Stephen—my stepdad—he's brilliant. He met Mum before we . . . before I was born, and he's been there for us, right through everything." She pushes the hair back from her face. "So what does your mum think of your dad still acting all tough—or didn't you tell her?"

"My mom's dead," I say.

It's funny. It's been ten years, but sometimes it can still hit me like it only just happened.

"Oh, I'm so sorry," she says. "I can see I've made you really sad."

"It's okay. You didn't know. It was a long time ago. I was only seven when it happened."

"But it's not something you ever forget, is it?"

I shake my head.

She looks down at her dog for a moment, then back at me.

"My mum's dead, too," she says. "It's part of why we moved here."

"What do you mean?"

Before she can answer, her dog stands up and yips. It's an odd, sharp sound, coming as it does from a dog with such a big chest.

"Oh, don't do that," Lainey tells her. "It's really annoying."

I want to ask her again what she meant—how her mom's dying made her and her stepdad move here—but the moment's gone. Asking now would just seem nosy and inconsiderate.

"My dad won't let me have a dog," I say instead. "I could have a cat, but I'm not really a cat person."

She grins when I say that, but I'm not sure why. It doesn't seem like it was particularly funny.

"He says it wouldn't be fair," I go on, "because I'm in school and he's at the store, and he doesn't want the store to smell all doggy. So if we had one, it'd have to be at home all day on its own."

"Yeah, Stephen won't let me have a dog either."

I look at the one standing on the floor beside her stool.

"Well, except for Em," she says. "But I don't really think of her as a dog. She's more like a, um, not-dog."

I smile. "You're weird. Cute, but weird."

"You think I'm cute?"

"You don't own a mirror?"

She lifts a hand and pulls at the mess of curls that spills every which way around her face.

"I think I look more like a mop-head."

"Then mop-heads have got to be the next 'it' thing," I tell her.

I stoop down and slowly move the back of my hand toward Em's muzzle. When people get bitten by a strange dog, it's almost always because they move too fast and seem threatening. I've been bitten—it was back when I was a little kid—and between the bite itself, then the stitches and the shots they give you, it's not fun.

Lainey's dog watches me with those brown eyes of hers, but she doesn't even sniff. When I get close, a faint growl rumbles in her chest.

"Em!" Lainey says.

I pull my hand back. I'm surprised, but not nervous.

"That's funny," I say. "I usually get along with animals— especially dogs."

Well, except for that one time.

"Oh, she's just a big grump today," Lainey says.

I sit back on my stool and check the time. Six o'clock. I can close now.

"You know, if you're feeling nervous," I say, "I'd be happy to walk you home."

"Really?"

"Sure. I just have to close things up here first." I pause a moment, then add, "But I do have to ask. Isn't your dog— Em, here—isn't she a good protector?"

The dog growls just then as though she doesn't like my using her name.

"Oh, she can be if she wants to," Lainey says. "But mostly she's just too lazy."

I know I'm just anthropomorphizing this, but I swear the dog gives her a dirty look before she lays her head back down on her crossed paws.

I get up, turn the OPEN sign to its CLOSED side, and lock the door.

"When did you move here?" I ask as I go back behind the counter again to open the register.

"About a month ago."

"Really? I haven't seen you at school."

"That's because Stephen homeschools me."

I nod. That's not so unusual around here. There are lots of old hippies living outside of town who homeschool their kids. Sometimes I feel sorry for them, because they miss out on hanging around with other kids their own age. But then they don't have to deal with all the social cliques and crap, so maybe it's not such a bad thing.

"Just give me a few moments here," I say.

Lainey watches me as I count out a float for tomorrow's till. I tear off the day's receipt tape, and write the date on it, then put it and the extra cash into an envelope. That'll go in the safe in the back of the store. Lainey waits while I put it away and get my coat. I set the alarm and kill the lights, and then we're out on the sidewalk and I'm locking the door behind me.

"Do you work here every day?" Lainey asks.

I smile. "Pretty much. It lets Dad go on his house calls so that he doesn't have to do it in the evening so much."

"What's a house call?"

"That's when people have stuff they want to sell, but it's too much for them to bring it all into the store. So Dad goes out to their houses. It's usually older folks, or people with big vinyl collections."

"I think it'd be a cool job," she says. "All this music."

"I guess it's not so bad. I can get my homework done if it's not too busy, and this time of year, it's never too busy."

I look up and down the street, but there's no sign of Johnny or the Millers. I saw them leave while we were talking earlier, but half expected them to be hanging around somewhere nearby at closing time.

"So which way do we go?" I ask.

She points up the hill to the Heights, the old part of town where all the original houses stand. Before they drained the marsh to make the sandy beaches and open water of

Comfort Bay on the west side of the point, the Heights was where the rich folks built their summer homes: high above the water, with boathouses and docks on the rocky shores below to house their yachts and entertain their guests. Now the rich own most of the shoreline along Comfort Bay, all the way up to the public beach, while the houses on the Heights grow more ramshackle every day. The old boathouses and docks have mostly been washed away.

"We live in that big place at the end of Lighthouse Street," she says.

"You mean the old Fairbourne B and B? Is your stepfather reopening it?"

I remember hearing that someone had bought the place and was fixing it up, but the idea still surprises me. The old stone building isn't as bad as some of the places up on the Heights, but it's been sitting there empty for a couple of years, and I can't imagine the work it would take to make it commercially viable again. And the *turistas* tend to stay in the new hotels near the public beach, or if they're looking for quaint without all the amenities, the Harnett Arms Hotel on the town square.

She laughs. "Hardly. The only company he keeps is with his books—the older and mustier, the better. I think the house used to belong to a cousin of his agent."

"What's he need an agent for?"

"He writes books. Nonfiction philosophy . . . historical stuff. Very dry and boring, but you still need someone to sell it for you, I guess." She looks at me. "So what do you do when you're not at the store?"

I shrug. "Not much. Hang with my friends, watch movies, listen to music, play video games."

"You don't read comics?"

"No, that's my dad's thing. I don't mind the early ones, but the ones they put out now are way too violent for me."

"Says the guy who plays video games."

"I'm more into the puzzle games like Myst, or this game I found on the Internet where there are hundreds of people online, playing in real time. It's very cool. And it's not just about shooting and hitting things. Your character has to . . ."

I trail off when she fakes a big exaggerated yawn.

"Well," I add, "if I was filling out a personal ad, I'd also put down long walks on the beach."

She smiles. "Because you *do* like them, or because those ads always say that?"

"Because I do. I spend a lot of time outside, walking around. The way the winds blow onto the East Shore is always good to clear my head." I glance at her dog. "That's why

I envy your having Em. What better way to spend a couple of hours than mooching along the beach with your dog?"

"I guess. I mean, I like it enough, but if that's *all* you do, it gets kind of old."

"Everything gets old if you do it too much."

"Oh, I can think of a few things that never get old," she says.

It takes me a moment to see that she's thinking the same thing I am. Then I blush, and she grins, which only makes me blush more. She reaches for my hand, but before I can take it, her dog gets in between us, making us walk apart.

"Oh, Em," she says, "are you jealous?"

I'm anthropomorphizing again, but I swear the dog gives her another dirty look.

"So do you have a lot of friends?" Lainey asks. "You must, from working in your dad's store."

"Not really. Dad's the real social person in our family—it's one of the reasons he does as well as he does in his business. He's genuinely interested in the people—not just their music and comics. I doubt there's a person in town who doesn't like him."

"Except for Johnny Ward."

I nod. "Only the Wards don't much like anybody, and I'm not *that* bad. My best friends are Chris Hayes and his girlfriend, Sarah. Chris lives right next door to me, so we're in and out of each other's houses all the time."

"But you don't have a girlfriend yourself?"

I'm not used to girls being so direct. I don't dislike it—far from it—but it's a little disconcerting, and I'm not exactly sure how to respond.

"Um, not really," I say.

"I bet you have lots of summer romances with the girls that come here on vacation."

I laugh. "You'd lose that bet. If I'm going to be with a girl, I like to think that there's the possibility it might last longer than a few weeks."

"Now that's something a girl likes to hear," she says. "Or at least this girl does."

Her dog bumps her leg, and it takes her a moment to get her balance.

"Oh, you're being bad today," she tells the dog. "Next time I go visiting, I just might not take you along."

"Do you always talk to your dog like she's a person?" I ask.

"Well, dogs are people, in their own way—don't you think? They sure have minds of their own sometimes."

"I guess."

We've talked our way almost all the way to the town square. At MacHatton Street, we turn left and start the steep climb to the Heights. Two blocks later we're turning onto Lighthouse Street, and Lainey stops. Her house is at the end of the block—the last building on the street, except for the ruins of the old lighthouse that rises up behind it. She turns to me.

"I can go the rest of the way on my own," Lainey says.

"That's okay. It's only another block."

"I know. It's just that Stephen—you know, my step-dad—he doesn't really like me talking to people. I'm only supposed to go out on the beach behind our house."

Uh-oh, I think. Having watched all too many after-school TV specials, I can see where this is going. Homeschooling. Not letting her go where she might interact with other people.

"No, it's not like you're thinking," she says, as though she can read my mind. "It's for our . . . it's for my own safety. There's just . . . um, people looking for us and . . . well, it's complicated."

"Lainey," I say. "If you need any kind of help . . ."

She shakes her head. "It's really not like that."

I don't know what to say. She doesn't look like she's being abused.

"Can I see you again?" I ask.

She smiles. "I'd like that. But that's complicated, too."

"Because I can't go to your house or call you?"

"Something like that. But I'm usually on the beach in the late afternoon."

"Okay," I say. "Maybe I'll take a walk there myself."

"That would be nice," she says.

Then she steps close and gives me a kiss on the cheek before she runs off the last block to the old B and B, her dog loping ahead of her.

I stand there, watching them go. I don't like this, but what can I do? I've no proof that anything terrible's going on, and Lainey certainly seems in good spirits for someone living in a terrible situation. So she probably isn't. But I still feel uncomfortable about it.

I watch until she reaches the gate of the B and B. She opens it, looks back and waves, then steps into the small yard in front of the house, closing the gate behind her. Then the stone wall around the garden hides her from my view.

I start to turn away when I realize I'm not the only person who was watching Lainey go back home with her dog. Half a block up, I see Johnny Ward standing in the shadow of somebody's house. He turns, and our gazes meet and hold for a long moment before he slips away. A few moments later I see him in the rocks above the house. He walks along the ridge, then takes one of the old stairways down to the shore, and I can't see him anymore.

Charles de Lint

I want to go tell Lainey that he was there, that she should be careful, but she obviously doesn't want me knocking on her front door. I watch the ridge for a while longer to see if Johnny reappears. When he doesn't, I finally turn around and head for home.

The phone rings as I'm starting to prepare dinner. I grab the receiver and hook it between my shoulder and my ear as I continue to work. I'm not doing a big spread. It's just a matter of warming up the spaghetti sauce I took out of the freezer this morning and cooking some pasta. I've also mixed a bit of crushed garlic with butter to spread on a loaf of French bread that'll go in the oven just before we eat.

"Hey," Chris says. "What's up, dude?"

Harnett's Point is on a lake, not an ocean, but Chris likes to think of himself as a surfer nonetheless. Sarah and I just smile and let him carry on with the delusion.

"Nothing much," I tell him. "I'm just making dinner."

"I came by after I left Sarah's house, but I guess you were still at the store."

"Yeah, Dad had a house call."

"Anything good come in today?"

I smile, thinking of Lainey. "Oh, yeah," I say, and then I tell him about her.

"Does she have one of those great accents?" he asks.

"She does. And she's totally gorgeous."

"Yeah? If that's true, then why's she hitting on you?"

"If you were here, I'd punch you."

"Dude, why do you think I'm saying this on the phone?"

"I might still come over there and punch you."

He laughs. "Nah. Then who could you brag to?"

"I wasn't bragging."

"Whatever. But Sarah's going to be disappointed to hear this. She was planning to hook you up with her cousin Ashley when she comes to visit next week."

"Oh, great."

"Don't worry. I'll tell Sarah so she doesn't sic her on you. But I don't know why you don't like Ashley. She's totally hot."

"Yeah. With an empty head."

"And that's a problem because . . . ?"

I smile, even though he can't see it. "Oh, Sarah's going to love to hear you said that," I say.

"C'mon dude. You know I was joking."

"I'm sure she'll understand."

"*Dude.*"

"I've got to go," I tell him.

"I am so dead," I hear him say as I pull the phone from my ear and push "End."

That night I dream of a forest. It's not like any I've ever been in before. I don't recognize any of the vegetation except for the ferns, only some of them are more like trees. Maybe they're a kind of palm. Some of the big trees have a reddish tinge to their bark, but most of them are grayish. They're all smooth, and the trunks rise twice the height of any trees we have around the Point. Some of them have woody vines that twist their way up the trunk until they almost cover the tree they're on.

The air is cool, heavy with moisture, and there's moss growing everywhere. The high canopy is so dense that almost no light gets through. Only a few sunbeams do make it all the way down to reach the forest floor, but their cathedral shafts of bright yellow make the shadows seem that much darker. I hear the sound of birds, high in the treetops, and catch the flash of bright colors: reds, yellows, blues, and greens that are almost fluorescent. Their song is like what you'd hear in a jungle, but this isn't like any Tarzan movie I've ever seen.

Oddly enough, I know that I'm dreaming, but my surroundings feel very real all the same. It's funny how you can make up a place in a dream that's so unlike anything you've really experienced.

I start to walk in between the trees, stepping over deadfalls and pushing aside ferns. Something breaks cover to my right, and I catch a glimpse of what looks like a kangaroo, except it's way too small, more the size of a cat or a small dog.

But now I know why I'm dreaming this, and where it came from: Lainey, and National Geographic specials on Australia. I'm dreaming of a rain forest, and it totally makes sense. I just hope Lainey shows up soon.

But she doesn't. I do sense something or someone watching me, but no matter how quickly I turn around, there's nothing to see. No one's there.

And then I wake up.

Dad's making breakfast by the time I step into the kitchen the next morning: eggs on toast, juice, and coffee. From the smell on his clothes I can tell he's already been out on the back porch for his first cigarette of the day. He's doing pretty good—down from a pack and a half a day to a half pack, often less. I still think cold turkey would be the way to go, but it's not my addiction, and he *is* cutting back.

"You know, the Fairbournes used to have quite a record collection," Dad says as he puts a plate in front of me. He goes back to the counter for his own, then sits across from me.

I can see where this is going, but I make him work for it.

"So I was thinking," he says. "If you see that girl again—"

"Lainey."

"Lainey, right. Maybe you could get her to ask her uncle—"

I smile. "Her stepfather. Were you even listening to me?"

"Sure, I was. But you know me. I've got no head for details."

Unless it's who produced some album made back in 1957, but I let it go. I mean, nobody's perfect, right?

"I'll ask her," I say, "though I don't know when I'll see her again."

He shakes his head. "Son, if you like a girl, you're supposed to get her phone number."

I didn't share my misgivings with him last night. I just told him I'd met Lainey and we'd seemed to hit it off.

"It's okay," I tell him. "It's not like I don't know where she lives."

After breakfast, I get my backpack. Dad's already waiting at the front door by the time I return from my room. He's looking down at our walkway.

"That's weird," he says.

I join him to see that he's looking at a set of muddy paw prints on the pavement. I backtrack them with my gaze, seeing that they come from the side of our house where my bedroom is. The mud's the same color as the dirt in the flower beds under the front windows.

"Now that's a big dog," Dad says. "Or at least it's got big paws."

I nod. The first thing that comes to my mind is Em, Lainey's dog, but I have no idea as to what she'd be doing here. Then I remember my dream, when I felt I was being watched in the rain forest.

I cut across the lawn and look around the corner. There are paw prints on my windowsill, as though the dog stood up to look in on me sleeping. It's dark enough in the Point that I don't need to close my curtains at night when I crank my window open a little to get some air.

"Looks like it was just mooching around," I say as I rejoin Dad on the walk.

"Doesn't seem right," he says, "a dog that big, skulking around on its own at night."

I nod in agreement, but I'm thinking, maybe it wasn't alone. I didn't see any footprints that might belong to a girl with red-gold hair, but then, unlike her dog, she might've been more careful where she stepped and just not have gotten mud on her shoes.

The big question is *why* she'd been here last night.

"Do you want a ride?" Dad asks. "I'm going out to the mall before I open to get some more packing materials."

Besides the store, Dad does a brisk business on eBay, selling his old vinyl. He sells comics online, too, but they don't do as well unless he's selling a full-issue run of some title.

"No, I'll walk with Chris and Sarah," I tell him.

I leave him to get into the pickup and walk next door to Chris's house. Before I knock on the weather-stained wood, I look back at our house again.

I'm not sure how I feel about Lainey prowling around my bedroom window at night.

I settle on the word Dad used when we first saw the paw prints. It's just weird.

In computer lab that day, I Google Australian flora and fauna, and the hits I get confirm what I thought I was dreaming about last night. The rain forest of my dream was made of the same eucalypt and paperbark forests I find pictures of on the Web. The names are as unfamiliar to me as the trees and vegetation were last night: gum trees and carabeens, tamborine and strangler figs. The figs are the massive things like vines that I saw choking the gum trees.

I find pictures of the palms and ferns, and then I find a picture of what I thought was a little kangaroo last night. And it *was* a kangaroo, except they're called pademelons.

I keep scrolling through pictures of Australian wildlife. The animals look as exotic as their names are strange: numbats and echidnas, wallabies and potoroos. And of course, that strangest Australian animal of all, the egg-laying platypus that can't make up its mind just what it is—mammal or duck.

Then I come to a picture of a dingo, and I stare at the screen.

It's like I'm looking at Lainey's dog.

The dingo looks exactly like Em.

Dingoes are wild dogs, the text tells me, not native to Australia. They were introduced four to six thousand years ago—which I figure makes them seem pretty much native by now, but what do I know? I'm no scientist. Because they interbreed readily with domestic dogs, their bloodlines are getting thinner all the time and there are few pureblooded ones left anywhere except for on some place called Fraser Island.

I guess they're like an Australian coyote—smart and clever and able to adapt quickly to whatever conditions they find themselves in. Apparently, they're quite fierce, which I suppose is an admirable trait for a wild animal. Unless you're a human and you run into one way out in the bush somewhere.

There's a link to another site with more pictures and information, but before I can click on it, the bell rings and I have to close my browser and head off to English class.

I catch Johnny Ward checking me out a few times during the day—in the halls between classes and again in the lunchroom. As soon as I look at him, he turns away.

I know it's got something to do with yesterday and my catching him spying on Lainey, but I have no idea exactly what. Johnny's a lot of things—a self-proclaimed tough guy, an indiscriminate bully—but he's never struck me as the stalker type. He doesn't need to stalk girls. There are always going to be ones who want to go out with the alpha male, even if he's only the alpha male of some dinky little high school like ours.

He doesn't try to approach me any more than he ever does since Dad barred him from the store. Usually he just ignores me. I think we both like it that way. I want to be left alone, and he doesn't have to lose face backing down from me because of what he thinks my dad would do if he hassled me.

He doesn't know that Dad feels kids have to sort it all out on their own. I've gotten into tussles with other kids, and except for hanging with the few friends I have, I pretty much go through my day with my head down and try to be ignored.

Dad always likes to tell me how it'll get better the day after.

"The day after what?" I asked him the first time he dropped this little pearl of wisdom on me.

"The day after you finish high school," he said.

Ha-ha.

I call Dad when school's out that afternoon. He doesn't have any house calls today and business is slow, so he tells me not to bother coming in.

I meet up with Sarah and Chris at Sarah's locker, and then the halls of Harnett High lead us out into the tail end of another dismal day. The overcast skies drizzle a misting rain that puts a fine wet sheen on everything, including us by the time we've walked half a block away from the school. Welcome to the Point in the off-season. I swear, the sunny days are all stored away until the summer, when they're brought out for the benefit of the *turistas*.

But it still seems like a good day to take a stroll along the east shore, maybe see if anybody's walking her dog out on the rocks. I tell Chris as much when he asks me if I want to hang with Sarah and him since I don't have to work.

"I have to meet this girl who's stolen your heart," Sarah says.

I laugh. "C'mon, Sarah. I've only just met her."

"And yet you have stars in your eyes."

"Okay, okay. So I like her. And just maybe she likes me. But it's way too early to tell where it's going to go, even saying it goes anywhere."

Besides, I add to myself, there's this matter of her skulking about outside my bedroom window last night.

Sarah gives me a light punch on my arm. "Don't you worry," she says. "Once she sees what a great guy you are, you'll be a shoo-in."

It's good to have friends. Maybe they're full of b.s. sometimes—because there's no automatic guarantee Lainey would want to be my girlfriend—but it's nice to have someone else think it's possible.

"I don't know about that," I say, "but you're right about me liking her as much as I do. Which is totally weird, since I've only just met her."

"Dude, I totally know what you mean," Chris says. "The first time I saw Sarah, I just knew she was the one."

Sarah gives him a playful shove. "You knew no such thing. We were six years old."

"I'm telling you, I totally did."

She holds up her right hand, fingers spread, and adds a digit from her left.

"Six," she says.

He shrugs. "I'm just saying . . ."

I know they say high school couples don't last, but Chris and Sarah have been together since we started Harnett High, and I believe they'll stay together. They don't *look* like they should work. Chris has an unruly tangle of brown hair, and wears baggy pants, T-shirts, and an oversize jacket—and that's just in the cold weather. Before any sane person thinks it's warm, he's walking around in short sleeves, shorts, and sandals.

Sarah, in contrast, always looks tidy. Her black pageboy never seems troubled by the wind, never frizzes in the rain. Her dresses are sleek, her jeans torn only if they're supposed to be. And when it's still cold, she bundles up along with the rest of us sane people.

She kisses Chris to shut him up, then turns back to me.

"I wonder what it's like being homeschooled," she says. "I think I'd go crazy if I had to sit at the table all day with my little brother."

"Yeah, and *why's* she being homeschooled?" Chris says. "Did she look like a hippie?"

"People get homeschooled for all sorts of reasons," Sarah tells him before I can say anything.

"They're all hippies in Hooper Valley."

"And some of them live in teepees—so what does that prove?"

Hooper Valley is where the communes sprang up in the late sixties, early seventies—hippies buying up the cheap property and going back to the land. Surprisingly, many of them stuck it out, and there are three generations living out there now. Most of them are artisans and make their living selling pottery and paintings and crafts to the tourists who flood the Point in the summer.

And like I said, not many of their kids bus in to Harnett High.

"That hippies are homeschooled," Chris says.

Sarah shakes her head. "All trout are fish," she begins.

"Which is why you don't find them in trees," Chris breaks in before she finishes with the usual, "but not all fish are trout."

It goes on like that as we walk up Main Street. We wave

to my dad as we pass his store, then Chris and Sarah turn off to go to her place while I continue to the town square. I cut across the little park with its bandstand and empty flower beds, and then I'm in the parking lot on the edge of the beach.

Now that I'm actually doing it, I'm feeling nervous. Sure, Lainey told me where she'd be during the afternoons—she as much as invited me to join her—but what if she was just being polite? What if she doesn't actually expect me to come?

And no, I haven't forgotten the paw prints outside my window. But just because that was weird doesn't mean I don't want to see her again.

After leaving the parking lot, I make my way across the public beach at the end of the Point. Pebbles and debris crunch under my shoes as I head for the path below the old lighthouse. The path takes me into the rocks at the base of the lighthouse, and then it splits in two. The one on the left goes to the rusting stairs that lead up to the lighthouse. I take the one on the right, down to the stony beach of the east shore.

I scan the beach, but everything's gray: the sky, the lake, the rocks and stones. There's color to be found, if you look hard enough—a speck of mica in this rock, a vein of pink quartz in another. But a cursory glance at the scene makes it feel like every bit of color's been sucked out of the day. Then far down the beach, I see two splashes of sunshine: Lainey's red-gold hair and Em's matching fur.

I start across the beach in their direction, but they don't notice me until I call out a hello. Em raises her head, then charges in my direction.

Oh, boy.

Don't show your fear, I tell myself, but it's hard not to. She's big, and no doubt strong, and I know she doesn't like me. But then I realize her tail's wagging like crazy. When she gets to me, she bangs her snout against my crotch, and I stagger back.

"Whoa," I say.

I quickly crouch down, but then she's licking my face.

"For God's sake," Lainey says as she approaches. "Don't be such a slag."

I'm not sure if she's speaking to Em or me. "A what?" I say.

"A slut."

There's something different about her today, and I'm not sure what it is until I realize that I get the feeling she's really not that happy to see me. Yesterday, everything felt close and warm, even though we'd just met. Today, it's like there's a glacial distance between us.

"So, it's good to see you," I say, standing up.

Em remains glued to my leg, pushing her snout against my hand so that I don't stop petting her.

Lainey nods, but doesn't respond otherwise. I'm starting to feel really awkward about being here. I feel like an intruder.

"You said you came out here in the afternoons," I try.

"And here I am."

Em leaves my side to yip at her, then immediately glues herself back against my leg to nuzzle my hand.

"Well, this is new," I say. "Yesterday she didn't seem to like me at all."

"You know dogs. They can be so fickle."

Actually, never having had one myself, I always thought they were supposed to be true-blue and loyal.

"Was there something you wanted?" Lainey asks.

"Just . . ."

Just to see you, I think, but obviously it had been a big mistake.

Could I have gotten my signals more crossed? Maybe she hadn't really been flirting with me yesterday. Or if she had, she'd changed her mind in the meantime. Could be she didn't like the way I slept, although playing Peeping Tom seems to have raised me considerably in Em's estimation. She's as friendly with me as Lainey is distant.

I shrug. "No, I just saw you down here on the beach and thought I'd come say hello. I should go."

That's her opportunity to say, No, stay, I'm glad you came, but all she does is nod in agreement.

"Okay," I say. "So long, then."

I give Em a final pat, and turn away. I hear Em growl, but when I turn to look, she's growling at Lainey, not me. I start to say something, then think better of it and head off again.

I hear claws scrabbling on the rocks behind me and Lainey calling, "You get back here!"

I turn again to see that Em's following me.

"I swear," Lainey tells the dog, "you get back, or I'll tell the old cheese all about your newest obsession."

The dog gives me a mournful look, then returns to Lainey's side. Her joyous body language when she first saw me is diminished to a slinking pace, head lowered, tail drooping. She turns to give me a last look, then it's back to Lainey, her upper lip lifting in a small snarl.

"Was there something you still wanted?" Lainey asks me.

I shake my head and return down the beach. If I had a tail like Em, I'm sure it would have hung between my legs.

That night, I'm back in the rain forest again. I wander slowly under the gum trees, shivering a little because of the cool damp in the air. All I'm wearing are the T-shirt and pajama bottoms I went to bed in. At least I'm not having one of those weird naked dreams that show up from time to time. The ground is squelchy, and my feet are soon wet and colder than the rest of me.

I can't figure out why I'm here—especially not after the way Lainey so emphatically blew me off this afternoon.

It doesn't make sense, except when do dreams ever make sense?

This one sure doesn't. I mean, there's nothing bizarre about it. I'm not on a roller coaster that suddenly goes under my desk at school to come up out of the wading pool by the public beach in the bay. Or chasing reindeer the size of mice around the store. I'm just in an Australian rain forest—*really* in it. Or at least it feels very real.

I stand there, looking through the trees for some clue, when I see something coming through the brush toward me. I stay quiet, hoping for another glimpse of last night's pademelon, but then I see it's just a wild turkey. It's about the size of a domestic rooster, with dull blue-black feathers, a leathery red face, and a yellow wattle. Because I'm not moving, it's almost upon me before it realizes I'm here.

It jumps back, and I hear someone say: *Bugger me, you gave me a start, mate.*

It's a male voice, with a strong Australian accent. I'm turning around to see who it belongs to when I realize that I heard the words in my head.

I turn slowly back to the turkey.

"Did you . . . did you just talk to me?" I ask.

The turkey cocks his head. *No, I was talking to some other great big lug, skulking about in the forest.*

"But I can't see your lips move."

I don't have lips, yobbo.

"No, um, you don't, do you . . ."

A talking turkey. Well, of course. If I'm going to dream, I might as well dream about a talking turkey.

I sit down on my haunches so that I'm not towering over him.

Are you lost? he asks.

"I . . ."

Lost? Do you really get lost in a dream, since it's not real? But I can't tell him I'm dreaming. Dream creatures probably hate to be told that you're just making them up, so I look for something else to say. Then I think of Lainey.

"I'm looking for this girl," I begin.

Aren't we all, mate.

"No, I mean a particular girl."

Of course you are. I can almost hear the lecherous wink in his voice. *So what's she look like?*

40

"She's got red-gold hair, and she's really pretty, and, um, she's got a dog that looks . . . well, it looks like a dingo, I suppose."

Word to the wise, mate. You don't want to mess with Dingo. He's full of aggro, that one, always spoiling for a fight.

"No, the girl I'm looking for has a pet dog that just looks like a dingo."

The turkey shakes his head. *You're new to the dreaming, aren't you?*

"I guess you could say so . . ."

I'm certainly new to dreaming when I know I'm dreaming.

Well, that's the thing about this place. Once a fellow gets a hook into you, there's no pulling it out again.

"I don't think that's really the case here—"

Take my advice, mate. You stay wide clear of Dingo. Get in his way, and before you know it, you'll be up a gum tree with no way back down again.

Before I can ask him what he means, he scurries off into the bush and I'm left standing there on my own.

That was weird, I think.

As I stand up again, I lose my balance on the wet ground. I start to fall, but before I land on the ground, I wake up and I'm lying in my bed, staring up at the familiar ceiling of my bedroom.

There's a weird sound in my room. I lie there trying to figure out what it is, until a crack of thunder sounds right above the house. Rain. Serious, heavy rain. I sit up and look at the window, and then I see the dog looking in at me from outside. It's tawny-colored, like Lainey's Em, but bigger, water pouring over its fur.

I want the girl, a man's voice says in my head, the tone deep and rough.

I know it's the dog speaking, but I also know that's impossible, because I'm awake now and animals don't talk in the waking world.

The dog drops out of sight, and I let out a breath I wasn't aware of holding. But before I can relax, I catch a blur of tawny fur, and then the dog's crashing through the window, spraying water and broken bits of glass and casement everywhere.

The dog lands on the bed, straddling me before I can move. Water drips from its fur onto my face.

She was promised to me, the voice growls in my head.

The air reeks of wet fur and something else—a deep, musky smell. The dog's snarling face is inches from my own. I get my hands untangled from my bedclothes, but before I can get them free to push the dog away, I wake up again.

There's no storm, no broken window, no shattered glass all over my bedroom floor. There's no big dog—standing

42

over me on my bed, or anywhere else that I can see. My face and bedclothes are dry.

I only dreamed that I woke from the rain forest dream. It's totally obvious. But still . . .

I get up and leave my room. In the front hall, I put on my coat and a pair of boots, then step out into the chill morning air. There are no new paw prints on the front walk. When I go around the side of the house to my bedroom window, there are no fresh marks in the dirt under it or on the sill.

Only a dream.

A dream within a dream.

I don't mind the rain forest—it's kind of interesting in a PBS nature special meets Disney sort of a way—but that last one has me shivering long after I've locked the front door behind me and returned to my bed.

I don't think I can go back to sleep, but before I know it, it's morning. I must have drifted off. But at least I didn't have any more dreams, or if I did, I don't remember them.

Chris and Sarah commiserate with me on the walk to school the next morning. I had to tell them about how Lainey blew me off yesterday, because the first thing they wanted to know was how things had gone with her.

"I feel like going right up to that house and slapping some sense into her," Sarah says.

"No you don't," I tell her.

Chris sighs. "Dude, this just sucks."

"Yeah, it really does."

We walk for another block in silence, Sarah and I with our collars up against the wind, Chris with his jacket open and flapping against his chest. You know what's really unfair? He never gets sick.

"My cousin's still coming next week," Sarah says.

All Chris and I can do is look at her.

"What?" Sarah asks. "I'm just saying. Ashley's fun."

Chris nods. "Yeah, dude. Fun's not the worst thing in the world."

"It's not the same," I tell them.

"Of course it isn't," Sarah says. "I'm sorry. I shouldn't have brought that up."

"It's okay."

"Are you working after school?" Chris asks.

I nod. "Yeah, Dad's got a bunch of errands to run."

"Well, maybe we can get together tonight—catch a movie or something."

"I downloaded this week's *Veronica Mars*," Sarah says.

Stations like the CW are available in the Point, but none of our families have premium cable packages or satellite dishes. If it wasn't for the high speed Internet that we do have, the three of us would be living in a cultural waste-land.

"That could be good," I say.

But I'm only mouthing the words. I appreciate their ef-forts to cheer me up, except I don't see myself cheering up any time soon. I know, I know. I only just met Lainey, but it feels different. It feels like we were supposed to be together, that our first connection in Dad's shop was the start of something more, something special.

And it's never going to happen now.

I'm working on a box of sixties albums that Dad left for me to price, when the door opens and in walks Lainey, Em on the leash beside her. She's still cute as a button, but the easy confidence she carried the first time she came into the store has been replaced with a kind of scared shyness, like I'm going to bite her head off for coming in. Considering how she treated me yesterday, I guess she should feel nervous. I should be angry. But I don't have the heart for it. And I hate seeing her look this way.

Still, I'm not going to make it easy for her, because she's got to know that treating me like that was not cool.

"You're pretty much the last person I expected to see

in here today," I say. "In fact, I didn't think I'd ever see you again, except from a distance."

"I don't blame you. I feel terrible."

"So what was up with the cold shoulder?"

I come around from the counter and bend down to pat Em, but she backs out of reach behind Lainey's legs.

What is it with these two? They're either hot or cold, with no middle ground.

"I'm so, so sorry about yesterday," Lainey says. "The afternoons are supposed to be mine—I mean, they're the time when I get to . . ." Her voice trails off and she sighs. "This is so hard to explain, so I'll keep it simple. I guess I was just having a bad day, and unfortunately, I took it out on you. It won't happen again." She looks down at her dog, then back at me. "Or at least I'll try my hardest to make sure it doesn't. Sometimes I just get . . . moody."

Oh, oh, I think, as I get this sudden flash of insight. This smacks an awful lot of some kind of bipolar disorder, or multiple personalities. Maybe that's why she's being homeschooled. Not because her stepfather's a control freak, but because he can't be sure who's going to be home inside her head on any given day. Maybe there's more than the two personalities I've met so far. Maybe some of them get violent.

Do I have a hyperactive imagination? Well, yeah. But it's all possible, right? So does it give me pause? Sure. Is it going to stop me from wanting to see her? Not a chance.

It's not just because she's cute and bright and has this energy that seems to crackle in the air around her. It's because of that moment when she stepped into Dad's store two days ago. Something happened to me then that made a connection. Maybe not from her to me—maybe she doesn't feel what I do—but the connection's definitely there from me to her.

I've had girlfriends before, and we're not even in that kind of relationship yet, but I've never felt this strong of a connection to a girl before.

"It's okay," I tell her.

"No, it's not. It was really mean. I *asked* you to come see me on the beach."

"Okay, it was mean. But let's put it behind us."

"Really? That would be so brilliant."

If I hadn't already wanted to do so before, the glow of happiness and affection that flows over her would sure make me want to now.

"Really," I tell her.

She steps close and gives me a hug, and I feel everything else in the world melt away until there's just her, here in my arms. But then Em pulls on her leash, tugging Lainey's arm away, and we break apart. Lainey frowns at the dog and drops the end of the leash that she's holding on the floor.

"Don't be such a show pony," she tells the dog, then she looks back at me. "Can I stay a little while, or are you busy?"

"I'm just pricing stock," I say. "It can wait."

I go back behind the counter and she sits on the extra stool, the dog flopping on the floor between us.

I wonder if there's some way I can bring up the question of medical problems—just so that I can get a feel for what I'll be dealing with—but right at this moment, I can't see any way to do it without making her feel bad. So I stick to safer subjects.

"You didn't strike me as the sort of person to be into endorsements," I say.

She's wearing black tights and clunky black boots with an oversize brown Roots sweatshirt that hangs halfway to her knees. Her hair's pulled back into a loose ponytail, but it still looks like a halo of sunlight framing her face.

"You mean this?" she says, grinning as she taps the logo. "It's just a bit of a laugh. Root's a fairly impolite word back home."

"What's it mean?"

She shakes her head. "I'll let you figure it out."

"I'm not even going to try."

"Wuss."

By Lainey's stool, Em thumps her tail on the floor as though in agreement.

I have to stop anthropomorphizing this dog, but it's hard. Then again, what do I know about dogs? Who knows what goes on inside their heads.

"Do you miss being away from home?" I ask.

"This is my home now," she says, "but yeah. It was different there. For one thing, the weather was better."

"We save up the sunshine for the summer when the *turistas* take over the town."

She smiles.

"So do you miss anything?" I ask.

"The birds—I don't see as many, and they seem drab compared to ones like our lorikeets and crimson rosellas. And I really miss the trees—the big old gums, and the massive figs, where each one's like its own forest. Yours all seem so much smaller."

I remember the towering trees in my dream forest and think, she's right about that.

"What about your friends?" I ask.

"I didn't really have any. We lived out in the bush, and we were always moving around, so we were never anywhere long enough. Stephen was sort of a game warden back home,

49

so we'd camp in all these out-of-the-way places in the bush, keeping a watch out for poachers."

I find it odd how she refers to her stepfather as Stephen. If Dad remarried, would I do the same with my new stepmother? Probably, I realize, because it would be impossible to call her Mom. But Lainey doesn't have the same affection for her biological father, seeing how he abandoned her before she was even born.

We start talking about music we like then, and movies and TV. She's a recent convert to film, since she didn't have access to it when she was living in the bush—something I can't imagine. Now, she tells me, she devours anything she can get her hands on.

I want to talk about this condition of hers, but I manage to let it go for some other time. That leaves the business with the tracks outside my windows. I know it's ridiculous, but because I have this paranoia that Em understands everything we're saying, I feel the need to get Lainey away from her dog for a moment.

"Hey, I want to show you these new CDs we got in today," I say. "I think they're all Aussie bands—at least the CDs were made there. I've never heard of any of them before."

I get up and lead her to the back of the store where the CDs are. Em stays by the counter, curled up on the floor beside Lainey's stool.

When I show Lainey the CDs, she pulls one out.

"Oh, Little Birdy," she says. "I love this band."

"Maybe I'll take it home and give it a listen."

"Oh, and you need to take the Veronicas, too," she says, pulling out another couple of discs and handing them to me. "And Killing Heidi."

"Don't they sound friendly."

"No, it's just their name. They're really good. Sort of crunchy pop. And try this one, too."

I look at the cover of the CD she hands me. The band's called Rambling House.

"They're more folky," she says, "but I've seen them live and they're brilliant."

I glance back to the front of the store. Em hasn't moved. I turn so that my back's to the dog and pitch my voice low.

"This is going to sound weird," I say to Lainey, "but do you let Em run out on her own at night?"

"What do you mean?"

When I explain about the paw prints we found outside my window and on the sill, she gets a horrified look.

"And that's not the only weird thing," I say. "The past two nights I've been having these dreams, like I'm in Australia—where you know I've never been—but the details are so—"

51

She puts a finger to my lips. "No more," she says. "And please . . . don't talk about this around Em."

"Now see, that's still more weirdness. That's why I brought you back here to talk, but she's just a dog, right, so why would it matter what I say around her?"

"It does," Lainey says.

"Okay, now that's begging for an explanation."

She nods. "But I can't right now. Please, just promise me you won't talk about this to anyone."

Those big brown eyes settle their gaze on mine, and how can I say no?

"I promise," I say. "But you really need to tell me what's going on. Is she wearing a wire or something?"

"A wire?"

"You know. A hidden microphone—like in all those cop shows."

She smiles and shakes her head.

"Can you come to the beach tomorrow afternoon?" she asks.

I nod. "But not till around five."

"Meet me there tomorrow, and I'll tell you everything."

She and Em leave not long after we return to the front of the store. I'm mad at myself as I watch them walk off down the sidewalk. Why did I have to go bring that up? She probably would have stayed until closing and I could've walked her home. Or at least as far home as she'd let me.

Now I only have tomorrow afternoon to look forward to, and I can't pretend I'm not feeling a little apprehensive, considering what happened the last time I met her on the beach.

But that's the problem with words. Once you let them out of your mouth, there's no taking them back again.

It's Dad's turn for dinner, and he brought home a pizza from Mario's. He puts it on the table along with a salad he's tossed together from what we had in the fridge. Mushrooms, spinach, and some grated Parmesan with a light oil dressing. I look at him where he sits across the table from me, wearing his NEVER MIND THE BOLLOCKS T-shirt. There're kids at school who'd love to wear it, but I can't think of a single grown-up.

"So, I was wondering," I say. "Did you ever go out with a girl who couldn't let her parents know she was seeing you?"

He laughs and serves us each a slice of pizza.

"It was the story of my life," he says. "But I wasn't a good kid like you, son. I'd already left home by the time I was your age. I was riding with a gang, wearing their colors." He shakes his head. "Not exactly the kind of boy a girl could bring home to meet her parents. And I always had a thing for good girls, so yeah, more often than not, I didn't meet my girlfriends' parents way more often than I did."

"Didn't it feel weird to you?"

"At the time . . . not really." He looks past me for a moment—losing himself in a memory, I guess, because then he adds, "But I suppose it should have. I know it sure would now." His gaze comes back into focus and he looks at me. "So, where's this going?" he asks.

"It's Lainey," I tell him.

He nods.

"I think she really likes me," I say, "and I know I like her, but I can't go over to her house, or call her, or anything. Her stepfather doesn't let her see *anybody*. She's homeschooled, so she doesn't even go to school."

"That's . . . different."

"Try not normal."

"C'mon, Miguel. We're both open-minded enough not to expect everybody else in the world to see things exactly the way we do. Did she say *why* her stepfather's got her on such a tight leash?"

I shake my head. "She said she'll tell me tomorrow."

"Then maybe you should give her the benefit of the doubt until then."

"I guess. But there's something about it that doesn't feel right."

"I can see why you'd think it was a little worrisome," Dad says. "Truth is, I'm getting a bit of that vibe myself. But I still think you should wait." He pauses a moment before adding, "Unless you think she's in immediate danger."

I shake my head.

"So give it until tomorrow," he says. "Now eat your pizza. I didn't slave over the oven all day just to watch you let it get cold."

"You didn't slave . . . you bought it."

"So I slaved over the till to earn the money to buy it. Same difference."

"Not even close."

We grin at each other. I help myself to some salad, then pick up a slice of the pizza.

My dad's so cool—I mean, if you get past the fixation on comic books. Chris and his dad get along really well, too, but I know he could never have this kind of a conversation with his. My dad's like a best friend, though that doesn't stop him from laying down the law when he feels he has to.

I guess I don't even mind him dressing like he's still a kid.

I go over to Sarah's after dinner to watch the latest *Veronica Mars* with her and Chris. Before we start, I tell them how

Lainey came into the shop to apologize this afternoon. Chris gives me an enthusiastic high five, and I get a big smile from Sarah. I don't tell them any of the weird stuff—like Lainey's reaction to what I told her, and then her not wanting her dog to overhear us. Like *my* not wanting the dog to overhear us.

I'd just as soon not keep secrets from them, but whatever's going on is Lainey's business. I figure she has the right to decide who gets to be a part of it and who doesn't.

But if she blows me off again tomorrow afternoon, all bets are off.

When I get back home, I'm nervous about going to bed—no surprise there, I suppose, considering my dreams last night. So I stay up late playing World of Warcraft until Dad finally comes in and says, "You remember it's a school night, right?"

He's not hard-line about my having a specific bedtime—hasn't been for years—but we both know that I'll be useless tomorrow if I don't get some sleep tonight.

I can't explain my reluctance, so I just nod in agreement and log off the computer. I take my time washing up, brushing my teeth, getting undressed, but finally, I can't put it off anymore, and I'm lying in bed, staring at the ceiling. Somewhere between being sure I'll never fall asleep and the morning, I find myself standing in front of the biggest tree I've ever seen.

The trunk has to be the size of a small house, but as I step toward it, I realize it's not solid. All these branches have bent down under their own weight until they've grown back into the ground, making new trunks. From a distance, it all looks like one, but now I see that I can walk right inside.

So I do.

I mean, it's a dream, right?

You know how in a horror movie people are always wandering off from their friends, or going down into the dark cellar, and you think, Don't be an idiot. Well, maybe life for celluloid characters is like a dream, because here I am, the idiot, blithely walking into this dark, weird place that could hold any kind of danger.

It was twilight outside. Here, it's a murky gloom. I can see, but not clearly. I walk around inside, marveling at how many of the branches growing into the ground are as thick around as the trunks of the spruce and pine back home. Then I get to the tree's main trunk. It's not quite the size of a house, but it's still huge. Ten of me would have trouble touching hands around it.

Once my eyes adjust to the poor light, I find myself sort of liking it in here. There doesn't seem to be anything spooky or dangerous . . .

Until I see the man's face carved into the trunk.

No, it's not carved. It's a living face made of wood growing out of the trunk. Because its lips move, and then I hear a male voice in my head.

You see how it is, boy? How'd you like to be stuck here?

I stare at the wooden lips, shaping the words, but the sound only resonates inside me.

"What . . . who are you?" I ask. I'm starting to feel sick to my stomach and realize it's because I'm so scared.

Why stop there? the face says. *Why not ask where, and when, and why as well?*

"What do you want from me?"

An eyebrow rises, quizzical. *I? You came to me, boy.*

I shake my head. "No, you . . . you brought me here. You want me here, and you want something from me."

I'm trying to sound brave, but I don't think either of us is fooled.

Well, aren't we the perceptive young man. Then the face in the tree stops smirking, and adds, *I want the girl.*

"The girl . . ."

Either she must come to me willingly, or she must be brought willingly to me by another. But come she must. She was promised to me.

"'She'? Who's this 'she' you keep mentioning?"

But I already know. It's Lainey. Who else could it be? I only started having these dreams after meeting her.

Don't play games with me, boy.

"Stop calling me that."

The face in the wood smiles. *Then what* should *I call you . . . boy?*

I start to tell him my name, but catch myself. I've read enough fantasy books to know that names are power. All the old stories say the same thing: if I give him my name, that puts me under his influence.

"Call me Jack," I say.

That's a good fairy-tale name. Maybe it'll bring me luck, because I sure need some. I need *something*.

This is nuts. I'm only dreaming. But if that's true, then why do I feel like this? Panicky and sweaty and scared out of my mind. Weak-kneed and nauseous.

I am *so* not hero material.

Well . . . Jack, the face says, *we both know who I want.*

"I'm just dreaming. I can't bring anybody to you."

You underestimate yourself. After all, you're here, aren't you?

"And . . . and where is here?"

Call it dreamtime.

I shake my head. "This is crazy."

It all depends on your perspective.

"What do you want her for anyway?"

The face smiles. *I don't want her. Just her blood. It doesn't need to be a lot.*

"What are you . . . some kind of vampire?"

Hardly. I just need her blood to be freed from my prison.

"There's probably a good reason you've been imprisoned."

I can feel the mental shrug. *Again, it depends on your perspective.*

"So why do you need her blood?"

We're related—cousins, you might say—and she's . . . pure. Her blood is pure. Most cousins of our breed have mixed their blood with others so much that they're little more than mongrels, but not her. I know her dame. I know her sire. She's the last of my cousins with a pure enough lineage to free me.

I know I'm dreaming. But I also know—don't tell me how—that this is more than a dream, too. Somewhere, someplace, it's real. Maybe it's because I know I'd never be able to come up with all this weirdness on my own.

I said I wasn't brave. And I'm not. I'm really not a hero. I've only role-played at being one in video games, and I usually get killed long before I hit the higher levels. But I know what my response to this has to be.

"I won't do it," I tell him. "I won't bring her to you."

You might live long enough to regret that.

I swallow hard. "I . . . I don't care."

We don't have to be adversaries. I can make it well worth your while.

"I don't want anything you could give me."

Are you sure? the face asks.

I nod.

And yet you will *help me. If not tonight, then soon.*

"I won't."

But he goes on like I haven't said anything. *I can make it easy for you . . . Jack . . .*

Suddenly I'm back in my bed, but I know I'm still dreaming because there's a woman straddling me who looks like she stepped right off the cover of some men's magazine: long silky hair framing an angel face, her body a nerd's exaggeration of an already well-proportioned woman.

And then there's the voice, in my head.

Pleasurable even, it says.

The woman reaches down and lays a soft hand on either side of my face.

Or it can be a nightmare.

And just like that, she's this gaunt, rotting corpse, with broken rib bones sticking out of her torso and maggots falling from what little flesh remains. The reek of death makes me choke and gag. And then she's grabbing my head and pushing it into her decomposed chest and—

I wake up screaming.

I'm sitting up in my bed, but the stink of the corpse still clogs my nostrils. My heart's pounding wildly, my body's slick with panic sweat.

The bedroom door bangs open and my heartbeat speeds up even more, but it's just Dad.

Please let it just be Dad.

Please let me be awake now.

Please don't let him change into some monstrous thing.

"Miguel?" he says, the worry plain in his features. He sits on the edge of my bed and pushes the sweaty hair from my brow. I'm holding my breath, but he doesn't change. He's still just my dad.

I'm awake.

"That sounded like one mother of a dream," he says.

I manage a nod.

"Are you okay now?"

"Yeah . . . I . . . I'm fine. It was just . . ."

I run out of words, and he musses my hair.

"Bad anchovies," he says. "Next time we have pizza, it'll be hold the little fishies."

I find I can call up a smile without having to try too hard.

"No, I don't think it was that," I say. "It was just . . . you know . . . a bad dream. No biggie."

"If you say so."

"I do. Thanks, Dad." I find another smile. "I guess we're never too old to need a hand to hold in the middle of the night."

Dad nods, and I see the sadness in his eyes that means he's thinking of Mom.

He musses my hair again and stands up. "A good trick," he says, "is to think of something you like as you're trying to fall asleep. Like . . . Lainey." Then he winks at me and leaves the room.

I wait until the door closes, but I don't lie back down. Not right away. I change my T-shirt, then stand at the window, looking out at the night.

I know it was just a dream.

But then why did it feel so real?

School's school, like it is every day, except today I can't wait for it to end so I can get over to the East Shore to meet Lainey.

And then there's Johnny Ward.

He seems to be around all the time, just on my periphery like he was yesterday, checking me out in the halls between classes. At lunch, when Chris, Sarah, and I are at our usual table, I keep catching him watching me from across the lunchroom. Whenever I look at him, he ducks his head, pretending he has no interest in me, but *something's* up, no question.

I find out after school.

Sarah has basketball practice, and Chris is doing his homework in the library so he can walk home with her later. That leaves me on my own as I step out of the school's front door into another gray day. But at least the drizzle's holding off.

I get as far as my turn onto main street when Johnny appears out of nowhere. He jerks his head toward the alley he stepped from.

"We need to talk," he says.

I look at him like's he just sprouted a second head.

"I'm serious, Schreiber."

"So talk," I say.

"Not here. Someplace where people can't see us."

He grabs my arm, and I pull loose.

"Touch me again and you'll lose that hand," I tell him.

I'm not as tough as my dad, and we both know it. But Johnny also knows that I won't back down, even if it does mean I get my ass kicked, and bullies prefer easier targets than someone who's going to fight back.

"Look, I don't know what she told you," he says, "but I wasn't following her. I mean, I was, but not for the reason you might think."

Just like when I met the face in the tree in my dream last night, I don't have to ask who "she" is.

"Oh, really?" I say.

"Can we please go someplace where we can't be seen?"

Johnny Ward using the word "please"? Did the world end and nobody bothered to tell me?

I look around, trying to spot the Millers, or maybe Johnny's older brother Dave. He's got to have somebody else lying in wait. But there's no one around—just the people you'd expect to see out on Main Street in the afternoon in the off-season, which is next to no one. I hesitate a moment longer, then follow him a little deeper into the alley.

"I know she chose you," he says, "and that's okay. I mean, I wish it was different—I wish she'd wanted to be with me— but it was up to her. You can't make someone like you. But you have to tell her, I would never have harmed her. I'd have thrown myself in the sea first."

Chose me? I think. What's going on here?

"It's funny though," he goes on. "That first time we met, we really hit it off. I thought she really liked me. We must have talked for hours. But the next day it's the cold shoulder and then—"

"Wait a minute," I say. "Where did you meet her?"

"Out on the East Shore. She was walking her dog."

"So what were you doing on the beach?" I ask. "Because the only thing I can think of is that you were shooting gulls with your BB gun, or sticking firecrackers in clam shells— neither of which is going to be all that appealing to a nice girl like she is."

I've seen him shooting at the gulls, but I've only heard about the firecrackers.

"It doesn't matter what I was doing there."

"Sure, it does."

He looks back at the mouth of the alley as though to make sure we're still on our own.

"I was sketching," he says.

"Sketching?"

He frowns. "You know, you put pencil to paper and try to capture the scene you see in front of you."

"I know what sketching is. I just can't imagine you doing it."

"Whatever."

"No, really," I say, unable to equate the tough guy bully with such an innocuous, not to mention creative, hobby. "How long have you been doing it?"

He shrugs. "I don't know. Forever."

I still can't believe it.

"Do you have anything you've drawn with you?" I ask.

"Give it a rest, Schreiber. That's not what I want to talk to you about."

"Do you?"

He gives the mouth of the alley another quick look, then reaches his hand inside his jacket. He pulls a small black book from his inside breast pocket and holds it for a moment before handing it to me.

I think my mouth falls open as I look at the beautiful seascapes and studies of rock falls, driftwood, and scenes around town that are captured on its pages. The pencil work is incredible—strong and emotional. Some of the sketches have watercolor washes that add to the beauty.

I remember going through a phase when I really thought I wanted to be an artist—not a comic book artist, which Dad would have loved, but a fine artist. Except I don't have the talent. I worked at it for months, but all it did was give me an appreciation for those who can do it. I know how hard it is to bring a scene to life and make it seem so effortless the way Johnny has on page after page of his sketchbook.

"These are incredible," I say. "Why would you want to hide something like this?"

"I'm a Ward," he says, as though that's supposed to explain everything.

"I don't get it."

"When I first got a sketchbook and started drawing in it, my dad beat the crap out of me and asked me if I wanted to grow up to be a fag."

All I can do is stare at him. I can't imagine my dad *ever* being unsupportive of anything I wanted to try, unless it was something self-destructive.

"But I couldn't stop doing it," Johnny goes on. "I just see everything in lines and light and shadow and need to get it down on paper. So I do it in secret. I've got dozens of books like that stashed away. I'm . . ." He looks around us again, as though still afraid that someone might be eavesdropping on our conversation. "As soon as I'm old enough, I'm leaving for the city, and I'm going to be an artist."

I shake my head. "If you're so . . ." I'm about to say "sensitive," but switch to "If you feel like that, why do you go around beating on everybody?"

"Because I'm a Ward. It's what's expected of me. And if Dad didn't hear that I'd been throwing my weight around, he'd beat the crap out of me again."

"Wow."

"You tell anybody, and you're dead."

"I won't tell anybody."

"I mean it. I don't care if your old man used to ride with the Devil's Dragon. You tell anybody, and I'll take you down."

"How'd you know my dad used to be a biker?" I ask.

"My old man asked around after I got kicked out of your store."

It never occurred to me that Johnny's father might have heard about him being barred from the store. If it had, I'd have been worried that he might take a run at Dad, because what would he have to be afraid of? There's the whole Ward clan to back him up—brothers, cousins, uncles . . .

"But since he doesn't ride with them anymore," I begin.

"C'mon, who are you kidding? Everybody knows how it goes. Doesn't matter if you're retired or not. Once a Dragon, always a Dragon. If my old man took yours down, the Point'd be swarming with bikers, looking for payback. My old man might think he's a big deal, here in the middle of nowhere, but even he's smart enough to know that's a war he could never win."

"I guess—"

"So are we done with the touchy-feely crap?" he asks.

"Sure, I —"

He leans closer to me. "Here's the deal," he says. "I just

want you to tell her that I won't hurt her—not ever. The dreams don't make any freaking difference."

This is the last thing I expect to hear.

"Wait a minute—"

"C'mon," he says. "I know you've been having them, too. It's written all over your face."

"It is?"

He laughs. "Of course it isn't, you moron. The guy told me. The face in the tree. He said if I wouldn't help him, he knew you would."

"Okay, this is really weird."

"Yeah, tell me about it. But here's the thing, Schreiber. I won't hurt her. But if you try to, I'll do more than kick your ass. I'll kill you."

I shake my head. "I could never hurt her."

He holds my gaze for a long moment, then nods.

"Yeah," he finally says. "I can see that. Or at least I can see you believe that. But people change, when push comes to shove. So I'm giving you a heads-up here. Don't mess this up. Em's a special girl. She'd be special even if some whack job that lives in a tree wasn't after her."

I just look at him.

"What?" he asks.

It's been bothering me ever since he mentioned how he

and Lainey had gotten along so well when they first met, but now I get it. He never met Lainey. He met the other personality in her head, who seems to be naming herself after her dog. But I'm not about to tell him that.

"Nothing," I say. "I was just thinking about her dog."

"Yeah—what's its name again?"

"Lainey?" I offer.

He nods. "That's one unfriendly mutt."

"I guess."

"So we're clear on all of this?" he asks.

Not even close, I think. This whole multiple personality thing is just too weird. But that's not what he's talking about, so I count the points off on my fingers:

"I take good care of Em. I don't tell anyone you're a secret artist. The dog's unfriendly."

"Don't you forget," he says. He starts to turn away, but pauses to add, "We're not going to be talking again unless you screw up."

"Suits me," I tell him.

I watch him go, my head swimming with information overload. You'd think the weirdest thing would be that Johnny Ward and I are having the same dreams, but it's not. It's the idea that he could possibly have a sensitive side. That he actually has a human side.

I track him until he steps around a corner, then I finally continue on up Main Street, heading for the East Shore and Lainey.

Or at least I hope it's Lainey who will be waiting for me there.

There's a strong easterly blowing in on the East Shore, driving spray from the waves up onto the rocks and shingles. I'm wearing a warm, insulated jacket, with a fleece underneath, but the bite of the wind still gives me a chill.

Instead of coming around by way of the Point as I did the other day, I've taken a shortcut by way of a couple of properties on Lighthouse Street. Once I've made my way between the houses, it's a quick scramble up through the brush and rocks on a makeshift trail that begins at the rear of their yards. That brings me to the ridge with the East Shore below, the beach spreading out to my right and left. It's all gray stone and gray water and gray sky. There's no flash of red-gold hair, but I start down to the beach anyway. I might just be early.

The trail drops here, cutting back and forth in switchbacks to deposit me finally on the loose stones at the bottom. I give a piece of driftwood a kick and shade my eyes to look into the distance, first one way, then the other. Nothing. Nobody.

Then a familiar voice calls from behind me.

"Over here!"

I turn to see Lainey standing on a big stone a little way down the shore, waving at me. She's wearing black cargo pants and a bright pink windbreaker. When I get to her, I see that she's found a little nook out of the wind, a big flat stone that's sheltered by the monolith rising up beside it. No wonder I hadn't seen her. She has a folded blanket on the stone and a small backpack.

"Hey," I say as I come closer to her.

I'm trying to check her out without making it obvious. Is this Lainey or Em? Or maybe she's got more than just two people living in her head. I don't really know much about how this business works with multiple personalities. But it feels like Lainey.

She raises her eyebrows. "Hey," she repeats. "That's the best welcome you can come up with?"

"I . . ."

Before I can say anything, she steps in, puts her arms around my neck, and pulls me close for a long kiss. My heartbeat's way into overtime by the time she steps back. She takes my hand and leads me back to her blanket.

"I brought us tea," she says. "Proper tea, with scones and Devon cream."

"Really?"

She smiles. "No, I just said that to get you all excited."

"You don't have to say anything to get me excited."

Her smile broadens into a grin.

"Later, boyo," she says. "First we have stories to tell."

I sit on the blanket and she settles beside me, legs drawn up under her, leaning half on me and half on the giant boulder that's protecting us from the wind.

"So what do you want first?" she asks. "Tea, or the story?"

Right now I don't want anything. I'm happy just to be here with her. But there's no sense in putting it off.

"The story," I say.

She draws away from me to sit cross-legged on the blanket, turned so that we're facing each other.

"Where to begin?" she says. But it's a rhetorical question that she immediately follows with, "I've got a twin sister."

If that's how she wants to explain it, I'm willing to play along for the moment.

"I know," I say.

Her eyes widen. "You do?"

"I met her on the beach the other day. She looks just like you, but she's not you."

"How did you know?" she asks.

"I didn't—not at the time. But thinking back, and then being with you in the store yesterday, I realized the two of you . . . I don't know . . . *feel* different from each other, even though you look exactly the same."

74

Well, of course they looked exactly the same. They were two personalities inside the same body. But that was for her to tell me, and I could wait. Except Lainey grins.

"Oh, this is going to make everything so much easier to explain," she says.

"How so?"

She ignores my question. "Except we don't look exactly the same. She's a half inch taller than me, and her eyes are a little bit of a lighter brown." Then she adjusts how she's sitting so that she can pull up the leg of her cargos to show me her right knee. "And I've got this little scar from when I fell out of a tree that she doesn't."

"Wait a minute," I say. "Are you telling me you *really* have a twin sister?"

She nods. "What did you think I meant?"

"That it was a . . . I don't know. I thought it was like a multiple-personality thing."

She laughs. "I'm sorry. I can see how you'd think that, but it still seems funny."

"So she's . . ."

"Oh, Em's real, all right, but then it gets a bit more complicated. We're shape-changers, you see. The only place we're safe—where we can both wear our human shapes—is in our house, so when we go out, we have to take turns being the girl."

I already know, from talking to Johnny, that the other personality—what I *thought* was another personality—calls herself Em. But from what Lainey's telling me now . . .

"Your sister's a *dog*?" I say.

"No, we're dingoes. And we can both take that shape. It's like I said, we have to take turns when we're away from the house."

This is so hard to process. I know I'm half in love with her, so I want to believe her. But what she's telling me is insane.

"I know how this sounds," she says, as though she knows exactly what I'm thinking. "I'm just hoping you have an open mind."

"I . . . I don't know what to say."

She nods. "I guess it's a lot to take in, but it's pretty simple, really. When we're in human shape, we're like you see us. We're just like anybody else—except we can change into dingoes."

"Dingoes."

"Right. But people don't know that. And when we're in our dingo shapes, people in this country just see us as some kind of scruffy dog—which is good because it means we don't really get noticed, but it's weird for us. It's so embarrassing to have to pretend to be dogs. I mean, think about it. We're dingoes, not dogs. Dingoes are the ancestors of all dog breeds. Why should we have to pretend to be dogs? We were here when Sun Mother walked the world into being."

"I don't know what that means."

"Oh, right. Over here you believe that Raven stirred the world out of that big old pot of his."

"Actually, I lean more to evolution."

"What's that?"

"What kind of homeschooling are you getting where you don't learn about evolution?"

"We're not really being homeschooled. We don't do school."

"So what do you do all day?"

She shrugs. "Since we moved here, we watch TV and movies. And we train."

"Train for what?"

"For whatever. To defend ourselves. To fight. We have to be strong and competent in both our shapes because we don't know which we'll be in when the trouble comes for us."

She flashes me one of her irrepressible smiles.

"I think we need to back up," she says. "You haven't even heard the story yet. When you do, it should all make a lot more sense."

In Crazyville, maybe, I think. But I just nod for her to go on.

"Back home there are lots of dingo spirits," she says, "but most of them have mixed blood. Em and I don't, because we were born on Fraser Island, which is pretty much the last place in Australia that our bloodlines run true."

"And that's important because . . . ?"

I ask because it's all beginning to sound a bit "master race" for my taste.

"Ordinarily?" she says. "It doesn't mean a thing. But Warrigal—he's the oldest of our clan. Some say he's the first dingo to step out into Sun Woman's world long ago, but I don't know about that. All I know is, he's old and powerful, and everybody just calls him Dingo, like he's the only one—though maybe it's only because he was the first. Anyway, somehow he got himself locked into a tree, and the only way he can be freed is by a pure-blooded girl pup like Em or me."

I kind of freeze when she comes to the bit about his being trapped in a tree. I think of last night's dream and the face in the bark telling me to bring her to him. The promises and threats.

It makes me wonder about Johnny's dreams. I never asked him for details, but now that I think about it, I'm sure they're similar to mine, except the face in his—if he had a face in his—would want him to bring Em to the tree.

Which is the same as bringing Lainey, I think, unless

there really *are* two of them, twin girls who can change into dingoes. But I know that's impossible . . . isn't it?

"You have a funny look on your face," Lainey says.

"I just thought of something, but it's okay. I'll tell you later. You finish your story first."

"Well, there's not much more to tell," she says. "He wants us so that he can get out of the tree prison—either as a mate or a sacrifice, it's not clear which, but either one's *eeuw*, right? Mum had already died when he started looking for us, so it's been up to Stephen to keep us safe ever since. But the place it gets complicated is that Dingo doesn't know that there are two of us. And neither does Tallyman—our blood father. Why are you smiling?"

"I don't know," I say. "It's just the name, I guess. It reminds me of how excited *my* dad was when he brought home an original RCA pressing of Harry Belafonte's *Calypso* from 1956—and I can't believe I remember that. Anyway, there's this traditional Jamaican song on it with the line, 'Come, Mr. Tally Mon, tally me banana,' and as soon as you said his name, I started to hear the song in my head."

She shakes her head the way I do when Dad's going on about some particularly arcane bit of musical trivia, then goes on with her story:

"The first time Tallyman came for us, we were in a bush

camp. I was sick and lying in the back of the camper, so he only saw Stephen and Em. They had a bit of a dustup—Stephen and our father, I mean—but Stephen got the better of him and then he and Em ran him out of camp, whacking him with sticks."

She smiles. "Em's got quite the temper. You should see her when she has a go at someone."

"So this, um, dingo guy, he wants either one of you?"

She nods. "Except this is where it gets more complicated. Like I said, he thinks there's only the one of us, that this dingo girl he senses is a powerful and pure-blooded pup, perfect for his needs. But Stephen's done a whole bunch of research about this, and he says it's only when the two of us are together—either as girls or dingoes—that we're strong enough for what Dingo needs. Each of us, on our own, isn't. So Stephen's worked up some kind of charm so that, when we're on our own, Dingo can't even sense us."

"But the two of you go out together all the time."

"Except one of us is a girl and the other a dingo, and then it's *like* we're on our own. It's only when we're both girls, or both dingoes, that he can sense us. The only place we can be together as girls, or dingoes, is in our house."

"Should I even ask why?"

She smiles. "It's because Stephen's got some other kind

of mystical thingamajiggy in place that blocks Dingo from being able to find us. A magical ward."

"This is weird."

"I know. Is it too weird?"

Too weird? I think. We passed too weird a long time ago in this conversation.

"I've been having these dreams," I say instead.

"That's what you said yesterday. Did you have another last night?"

I nod and go on to describe all three of the dreams in fuller detail than I'd been able to in the store. Lainey sighs when I'm done.

"Whenever people come into contact with us," she says, "somehow, Dingo knows. He still can't sense us, but he can sense the connection, so he tries to get at us through the person who's been with us."

"Through dreams," I say.

She nods. "Except dreams are different for cousins. It's a real place for us."

"Cousins?"

"People like Em and me, who only borrow our human shapes."

"So you're *really* dingoes?"

"Yes. But when we're girls, we're really girls. It's complicated."

81

"Everything's complicated," I say.

"But that's true for everybody, isn't it? We all just have different complications in our lives."

"I guess."

For a long moment, I look out at the lake and the choppy waves coming to shore, then turn back to her.

"So is it going to be like this for you for the rest of your lives?" I ask.

"It sure seems that way, and we hate it. Every time we meet someone we like, Stephen finds out and we have to move again. Coming to Harnett's Point is the farthest we've moved so far, but we've still moved about ten times in the last year and a half."

"So your stepfather's not just some weird control freak," I say.

She smiles. "Well, he is, but in a good way. It's for our protection. He promised our mum he'd look out for us when she was gone. The trouble is he's mostly a thinker, not a fighter. His idea of a solution to our problem is for us to spend our lives hiding."

"It's like you're in a Witness Protection Program."

"Which constantly gets blown, but yeah. That's pretty much it, and Em and I are sick of it. We talked it over last night, and we've decided that it's got to stop. We can't live our whole lives in hiding."

I give a slow nod of my head. I'm trying to digest all of this, but nothing she's saying is making it easy. She doesn't look crazy, but she has to be, doesn't she? Because things like this don't happen in the real world.

"So are you hiding from your father, or Dingo?" I ask.

"Both, I suppose. But Tallyman is the biggest danger, because he's free to roam around, while Dingo's stuck in that tree."

"Why would he do it? I mean, you're his kids, right?"

She shrugs. "I don't know. Stephen thinks Tallyman owes some sort of debt to Dingo and this is how he means to pay it. Or that he's doing it to curry favor. Tallyman wasn't with our mum because he loved her, or even because he just wanted to have sex. He was only there to make her pregnant, and then, when we hit puberty, he came looking for us."

"Though he thinks there's only one of you."

She nods.

"Why doesn't he just come and get you? *He's* not locked in a tree, is he?"

"Stephen's wards keep him from finding us."

It all sounds so plausible—enough so that I keep asking questions, partly because it's so fascinating, but, I hate to admit, partly because I'm trying to trip her up. Except she has an answer for everything, and nothing contradicts what she's already told me.

"Is Stephen a dingo, too?" I ask.

She shakes her head. "He's another canid cousin, like us, but his blood's too thin for him to shape-shift."

"Then who was at my window the other night?"

"It could only have been Tallyman. Dingo must have sent him." She cocks her head to look at me before adding, "I can't believe you're just listening to all of this."

"It's . . . surprising," I say. "But I guess I've already had a few weird experiences that are related to you, and this is helping me make some sense out of it all."

It's a white lie, because *nothing* makes sense right now. Sure, it all holds together, but it's based on things that can't be possible. I'm here only because I like her.

"But I don't know *why* you're telling it all to me," I say.

"I just wanted to be honest with you," she says. "And . . . well, if Stephen finds out that I've met you—that I'm seeing you, that Dingo's sending you dreams and Tallyman's been sniffing around your house—we'll have to move again, and I don't want to move. I . . . I really like you, and I think you like me, too."

"Oh, I do."

She nods. "It's like we have this connection. I felt it from the first moment I walked in your dad's store."

"You, too?" I say, but I can't help but wonder why there has to be all this other crazy baggage tied up with it.

I hesitate a moment, then have to ask, "So, um, can you show me?"

"Show you what?"

"How you change into a dog—I mean, a dingo."

She shakes her head. "If I do it away from Stephen's wards, Dingo will know where I am, and it'll call Tallyman right to us."

I see the disappointment in her eyes. It's probably mirroring my own, because of course she can't change into anything. She's a teenage girl, just like I'm a teenage boy, and no matter how we might want to be taller or thinner or fly around with wings, in the end we're just who we are, though I guess we both wish she was just a normal girl.

But it would have been so cool if she could do it.

It turns out she's disappointed for another reason.

"I thought you believed me," she says.

"I . . . I don't know what to believe. Sure it's weird that this stuff you've been telling me relates to the dreams I've been having, but . . ." I sigh. "It's a big jump from dreams to people literally changing into animals."

She nods.

"I *want* to believe you—" I start.

She breaks in. "No worries. I understand. It sounds crazy. *You'd* have to be crazy to believe it."

"You didn't let me finish," I say. "I was going to say that

while I don't know what to believe, I still want to help you. I still want to be with you."

"But—"

"That means I'm going into this as though everything you've told me is true, and we'll see where it takes us."

"Really?"

I nod, and I really do mean it, and not just because I'm a sucker for a pretty face. The connection between us feels real. It felt like that from the moment she walked through the door of my dad's store, and knowing now that she felt something, too, just makes it seem all the more meaningful.

"This won't be easy," she says. "I know it just seems like dreams, but you're in real danger from Dingo and . . ." She hesitates, then goes on. "And I'm in danger from you."

"From me? I'd never hurt you."

"I know that. Or at least I think I know that. And I'd go to him, if it meant you'd be kept from harm."

We've just met, and it's already life and death?

"But Stephen tells us over and over again," she says, "how Dingo can get into people's minds and make them do things they'd never do normally."

"That's not going to happen," I tell her.

I remember last night's dream and how helpless I was in it. But it was *just* a dream, and, no matter what Lainey might think, dreams can't hurt us.

But right now's not the time to argue what's real and what's not with her. I said I'd go along with her as though it was all real, and that's exactly what I'm going to do.

"So how can we make you safe?" I ask. "How do we stop them from chasing after you?"

"I honestly don't know. Em has some ideas, but she said she needs to find a chance to sneak one more look at one of Stephen's books first." Lainey hesitates a moment, then adds, "She says that Johnny has be involved."

"Johnny *Ward*? Are you kidding me?"

She shakes her head. "She really likes him."

"But—"

Lainey holds up her hand. "He's different with her. He's really . . . attentive and smart—not at all like you described him."

I'm about to protest some more, but then I think of my encounter with him after school, just before I came here to meet Lainey.

"Maybe I can see that," I say instead.

"You can?"

I nod. "He's been dreaming, too."

"That makes sense. There had to be a reason he was following me the other day. He must have thought I was Em."

I go on to tell about what he told me in the alley on my way here.

"That's good," Lainey says.

I raise my eyebrows.

"That he feels so protective toward her," she says.

"I guess."

"We should meet here tonight—on the beach. Will you bring him?"

"What do I tell him? He doesn't know . . . well, any of this stuff you've been telling me, does he?"

She shakes her head.

"So, what should I say?"

"I don't know. That Em needs him, I guess. Hopefully that'll be enough."

I nod and start to get up, but she grabs my hand and pulls me back down beside her on the blanket.

"It's still early," she says. "Do you have to go so soon?"

"I guess not . . ."

"Good," she says.

Then she leans close and lifts her face to mine so that we can kiss. As soon as our lips meet, I forget all my second thoughts about these crazy stories she's been telling me. I'm happy just to be here, and I never want to go away.

But of course, eventually, the afternoon draws to an end, and if we didn't have to leave anyway, the spitting rain that comes sends us each off on our separate way. Lainey gives me a last, lingering kiss.

"Until tonight," she says.

"I'll be here."

After leaving Lainey, I call Dad at the store and tell him I won't be home for dinner. I guess he's totally caught up in something—cataloging old vinyl, no doubt, or looking up some *Archie* comics in the price guide—because he just says sure and doesn't even ask me where I'll be. That suits me fine because if he knew where I was going, I doubt he'd be happy.

We don't have railway tracks in the Point—not anymore. The trains are all long gone, and the tracks have all been paved over and turned into jogging and biking paths. But if we did still have them, the Ward house would be on the wrong side. As it is, once I step onto Johnny's street, the buildings get shabbier and the lawns more unkempt. A big dog lunges at me from a yard and almost gives me a heart attack. But it's on a chain and the chain holds. What really creeps me out is that it doesn't bark. It just stares at me as I continue down the street, my pulse still going way too fast.

What is it about dogs, anyway?

I hadn't exactly lied to Lainey. I really *have* been after Dad to get one for years. But I'm also a little scared of them. I suppose I have good reason. That time I got bit as a kid?

It was by a big German shepherd that some yahoo let loose in the park where I was playing. Later, Mom—she was still alive at the time—said that the dog's owner must have been abusing it for years because dogs didn't just go after kids for no reason. But knowing that didn't help much.

I remember that dog coming for me. I remember turning to run, and then this explosion of pain in my leg when his jaws clamped around my calf.

Dad reached us before the dog could do anything else. He punched it so hard in the side of the head that not only did the dog let me go, but it stumbled to the ground and fell down. Then Dad punched the guy who'd let the dog loose in the park. I think he might have gone on to really hurt that guy, but Mom stopped him. She pulled Dad away once the guy had fallen down, and they took me to the hospital.

I don't think about that so much—I mean, it's not a memory I call up every day or anything. It's only at a moment like this, when some huge dog is looking to take a piece out of me and all I've done is passed by its yard.

When I get to Johnny's house, I look back. The dog's still sitting there at the end of its chain, staring at me.

I lift my hand, in a moment of bravado, and wave. Then I turn and walk up the driveway, stepping around a pair of junked cars until I can climb up onto the porch. The wood sags under my weight and I hold my breath, but it doesn't give way. There's no bell, so I knock on the door. There's no answer, so I knock again. After a few moments, the door swings open and Thompson Ward, Johnny's dad, is standing there.

Slouching in jeans and a sleeveless white undershirt, his pot belly pressing against the graying fabric, he looks like a fifties juvenile delinquent who got old and went to seed. He just stands there looking at me. His dark hair's greased back from his forehead and graying at the temples. He's got a long, lean face, pale blue eyes, and a thin line of a mouth. I've only ever seen him from a distance before. This close he reeks of cigarette smoke and alcohol. And danger.

"The fuck you want?" he says.

"Um . . . is Johnny home?"

"Do I look like his goddamn secretary?"

"No, I just . . ."

But before I can finish, he steps away from the door and waves a hand up a set of rickety stairs behind him in the hall. Then he retreats back into the living room where a ball game's playing on the TV. I stand in the doorway a moment longer, not sure what to do. Finally, I step into the hall. I glance into the living room and realize that, as far as Johnny's dad is concerned, I no longer exist. I hesitate a moment longer, then start up the stairs.

I call Johnny's name when I get to the top—not loud,

just enough to carry. A door opens, but it's not Johnny. It's his older sister, Sherry, leaning against her doorjamb, giving me a slow once-over. She's a couple of years older than me and out of school now, but I can remember seeing her in the halls. She'd perfected a cheap trashy look back then, and the tight tank top and cutoff jean shorts she's wearing at the moment tells me that she hasn't changed her image.

"Well, look what the lust fairy's brought me," she says. "And there I was, thinking I'd have to settle for my own hand."

Like pretty much every kid in school, I'd had daydreams about her during class, and more active fantasies alone in my bedroom at night. Back then, being the focus of her interest would have thrilled and paralyzed me. Today it just feels cheap.

"Is Johnny around?" I ask.

She tilts her head. "You don't like what you see?"

"I'm just here to see Johnny."

"So you're what? Gay or something?"

I'm about to say "or something," but then Johnny speaks from behind me.

"Take a hike, Sherry."

She gives him a salute with her middle finger and goes back into her room. I turn around to find Johnny scowling at me. I wasn't expecting a big welcome, but considering how we had a fairly civilized conversation earlier today, his animosity surprises me a little.

"What are you doing here?" he asks.

"We need to talk."

He shakes his head. "I think we did all the talking we need to do."

"Yeah, well, it wasn't my idea to come here," I tell him, "but Em asked me to talk to you."

The dark look in his eyes softens a little, though he's still scowling.

"So talk," he says.

I look back at Sherry's door.

He nods, then indicates the open door behind him.

"We can talk in here," he says.

"You know how bullshitty this sounds?" he says when I finish.

I shrug. "There's the dreams . . ."

He waves that off. "They're just dreams. They don't prove anything."

"Okay," I say, "then how about this. Maybe she doesn't have a sister. Maybe she's just a cute, crazy girl with a bunch of people living in her head. But she asked me to be on that beach tonight, so that's where I'm going to be. What about you?"

"What makes you think I care?" he asks.

I'm sitting on the edge of the bed, looking up at him where he's leaning against the windowsill. He's long since perfected a look of complete nonchalance, and he's playing it out now: sleepy-eyed, slouched with one shoulder against the wall, hands in his pockets. But I don't buy it.

"What makes you think I believe you don't?" I say.

A faint smile tugs at the corner of his mouth, there and gone again.

"So what're we supposed to do on this beach?" he asks.

"I have no idea."

"But you're still going to be there."

I nod.

"You've got it bad for her," he says.

"I know."

He doesn't say anything for a long moment. I look around the room, struck as I was when I first walked in at how it doesn't tell you much about the kid living in it. There's a bed with a threadbare quilt on it and a battered dresser that's seen better days, but those days were a long time ago. A faded Confederate flag hangs in the window as a curtain. The closet door stands ajar, but there's not much in the way of clothes hanging in it. There's a stack of car and music magazines on the floor by the bed.

And then there's the rifle hanging on the wall.

"If there's only one of her," Johnny says suddenly.

I pull my gaze from the rifle to look at him.

"That's the way it has to be," he says. "You know that, same as me."

"It's what makes the most sense."

"But when we know it for sure . . ."

His voice trails off, but I wait for him to finish.

"So, what happens then?" he asks.

He doesn't say it, but I know what he's thinking: Which of us is going to be with her?

"I think that's up to her," I say.

He gives a slow nod. "Yeah. I suppose it is."

Dad's watching TV when I get home and I'm struck with the difference between Johnny's father and mine. They're both watching the ball game, and Dad's got a beer, too, but he just looks like a guy kicking back after a day's work. Thompson Ward gave me the impression he was only killing time until he could hit something. Or someone.

Dad salutes me with his beer bottle.

"How was your day?" he asks.

"Busy. Speaking of which, I need to go out again a little later. Will that be okay?"

He gives me a dubious look. "It's a school night."

"I know. But I've got my homework done, and this is important."

Dad smiles. "Does this have anything to do with a certain young lady, recently moved into town?"

"Yeah, it's to see Lainey."

He doesn't say anything for a long moment, just studies me with sleepy eyelids that hide a mind that's anything but.

"Do her parents know?" he asks.

"It's just her guardian, and honestly? I have no idea."

He looks as if he's going to say one thing, but then changes his mind.

"All things considered," he says, "I'm the last person to say you shouldn't do this. But you need to be careful."

I nod, thinking, You have no idea how careful I have to be if everything Lainey's been telling me is true.

"I'm serious," Dad goes on. "Broken hearts are a lot different here in the real world. It's not like it is in some pop song, or a comic. But if you need to do this, then do it. I've got too many regrets of my own to stand in your way."

"What do you mean?"

He shrugs. "Everybody has chances that they passed up—things they missed out on. Did you know that your mother and I could have been together a lot sooner than we were?"

I shook my head.

"Oh yeah. We could have shared a lot more of that short life of hers, but I had things I thought I needed to do first. I wasn't ready to settle down. Didn't think I'd ever settle down. Except, you know what? I had this little voice in the back of my head, telling me different, but I was too pigheaded to listen."

"I didn't know."

"No reason you should have, son. All I know is, I wasted a lot of years that I could have had with her."

"I will be careful," I tell him.

"I know you will."

I meet up with Johnny at the end of Lighthouse Street. The sky's overcast and there aren't any streetlights here, so it takes me a moment to see the rifle he's holding down along his leg.

"Oh, man," I say. "Why did you have to bring that?"

"Do you have any idea what we're getting into?" he asks.

I shake my head.

"So maybe you can see my point in bringing along a little backup."

"Yeah, but a gun? Somebody's going to get hurt."

He shrugs. "Maybe. But it won't be me. Not without a fight."

"I don't think we're here to fight," I tell him.

"Whatever."

He turns away and starts for the path that'll take us down to the East Shore beach. I hesitate a moment. I look back across the town. You can see all the way out across Comfort Bay from here, a quilt of lights in the dark.

I have a bad feeling about this, but finally I turn around and catch up to Johnny.

"Change your mind?" he says over his shoulder.

"I never said I wasn't coming," I tell him.

We pick our way down the path. While my eyes have adjusted to the poor light, it's hard to make out much close to the ground. Still, we get down to the beach in one piece. The pebbles and stones make for uneven footing once we start walking toward the water. The only sound is the wind in my ears and the water lapping against the shore. It smells of weeds and fish and then I get a whiff of Johnny's cologne. I smile, until I remember the rifle he's carrying.

"Did anyone see you carrying that?" I ask.

"Would you relax? It's not like I was trying to sneak it into school."

"Yeah, but—"

"If anyone comes along, we'll just tell them we brought it to pop a few gulls."

Something he's certainly done before, but there's no point in arguing the right or wrong of that at the moment. Instead, I look around for Lainey. Or Em. Or maybe both.

Then the moon finally comes out from a break in the cloud cover, and I see them standing a little farther down the shore. It's still one girl and her dog, and the girl's Lainey. Don't ask me how I know. It's something in the way she holds herself, or how the dog sits quietly at her side.

I glance at Johnny, but even with the moonlight on his face, I can't make out what he's thinking. He turns to me.

"One girl and one dog," he says, echoing my thoughts.

"It doesn't mean anything," I tell him, trying to convince myself as much as I am him. "They could just be waiting for us to show up before—"

"Before what? The dog turns into a girl? This is bullshit, and you know it. I never should have come."

"But you're here now," I say before he can leave. "Let's see how it plays out."

He gives me a brusque nod, and we start down the beach to where Lainey and Em are waiting for us. Lainey smiles at me, her welcome plain, and I start to hurry forward to meet her, but Johnny grabs my arm.

"*She* decides," he says, his voice pitched low so that only I can hear him.

That's when I realize that he can't tell the difference between the two of them the way I can.

"This is Lainey," I say. "The one who likes me."

"Yeah? So when does Em come out to play? What the hell am *I* here for?"

He's raised his voice now enough that Lainey can hear him.

"Because Em says we need both of you," she says.

Johnny turns his glare from me to her. "And where's she?"

The dog gets up from where it's been sitting by Lainey's legs and walks over to him. She pushes her muzzle against the hand that's not holding the rifle.

There's never been much to like about Johnny Ward as far as I can see—even given the things he's told me. Still, something changes in him at the touch of the dog's muzzle. The tough veneer doesn't give way or anything. But there is a flash of tenderness in his eyes as he strokes the dog's head.

"I need some answers," he says.

His voice is quieter now—almost sad, I find myself thinking.

Lainey nods.

"Em's going to be here in a moment," she says, "and

then things are going to happen fast. You came here on good faith—can we ask you for just a little more?"

Johnny shrugs.

"Sure," I say.

"Thank you." She looks at the dog again, then back at us. "Em says that the only way we can be protected from our father stealing us away is if we're betrothed." She smiles. "Yeah, I know. That's kind of an old-fashioned word, isn't it? But this is something that goes back to before what we think of as old-fashioned was still new."

"You mean like engaged?" I ask.

She nods. "And it has to feel real. I know we've all just met, but you care for us, right? And we care for you. So when it comes up—and it's going to come up as soon as our father appears here—you have to agree without hesitation that we're betrothed. Miguel and me." She looks at Johnny. "And Em and you."

"I'm supposed to say I'm engaged to a dog?"

"A dingo, actually, but she won't be in that shape when our father comes."

He shakes his head.

"How does our saying that keep you safe?" I ask.

"Because if we're taken to Dingo unwillingly, the magic he needs to take from us won't work."

"I don't know if I can do this," Johnny says. "How am I

supposed to keep a straight face when I tell somebody I'm engaged to a dog—sorry, a *dingo*."

"I thought you cared for Em."

"I do. The *girl* Em, not a dog."

"She won't be a dog when our father comes."

Johnny lifts his rifle. "Why can't I just shoot him and be done with it?"

"Every death diminishes us," Lainey says, her voice more serious than I've ever heard it, "and killing kin . . . among the cousins, that can be the start of a blood feud that can last for centuries."

"Cousins?" Johnny repeats. "I thought he was supposed to be your father."

"That's just what they call other, um, shape-shifters," I say.

Johnny gives me a look. "Right."

I can tell he's as uncomfortable with the idea as I still am.

"So patricide's a big no-no?" he adds as he turns back to Lainey.

I'm surprised he even knows the word, but at this point, nothing about Johnny Ward should surprise me. Like Dad says—everybody's got hidden depths. Everybody wears masks. You just need to spend the time to get to know their story.

But I still don't like him any better. Or completely trust him.

"Think about it," Lainey says. "Parents are supposed to take care of their kids, not use them to pay off their debts. Families are supposed to *mean* something."

Johnny gives a slow nod.

"Except maybe that's all the more reason we should just pop your old man," he tells Lainey. "You know—get rid of at least one piece of trash."

His eyes are dark, and I know he's thinking of his own father.

"That would make us no better than him," Lainey says.

Johnny shrugs.

"Well," Lainey tells him, "I'd rather be putting something good back into the world than adding to its unhappiness."

"Maybe not shooting him would make me unhappy," he says.

Lainey doesn't say anything for a long moment. The two of them just stand there, looking at each other, as though they're having a conversation only they can hear.

"I can't stop you from doing whatever you want," she says finally. "But I'm asking you not to kill my father."

"I can live with that," he tells her. "For now. For tonight. But down the road? No promises."

"Thank you," Lainey says. She looks from him to me. "So, are we ready to do this?"

I nod.

"Bring it on," Johnny says.

I see a flash of—I'm not sure. Nervousness? Maybe fear?—cross Lainey's features, then she squares her shoulders and looks at the dog.

"Okay, Em," she says. "I guess there's no reason to put it off any longer."

I'm not sure what I was expecting. Even with the dreams I've been having, I never really bought into this idea that she has a real sister and that the two of them can change into dingoes and then back again. I just knew Lainey was in some kind of trouble and I wanted to help. And I know Johnny's bought into all of this even less than me.

But when Lainey turns to look at the dog, Johnny and I do, too, and then . . . and then . . .

I have to be dreaming.

I remember how real it felt when I met the turkey in the rain forest. When the face in the tree started talking to me. When the hot babe showed up in my bed and then turned monstrous.

All dreams.

This has to be more of the same.

I've fallen asleep and I'm dreaming all of this—maybe right from when Lainey came into the store. No, not that far back. But probably as far back as when Johnny took me aside in the alley and showed me his sketchbook, telling me he's an artist, because, really. How likely is *that*?

A lot more than this, I suppose.

Because a shimmer like a shivering mirage runs from the end of Em's muzzle all the way to the end of her tail. Every inch of her quivers, then she starts to rise up onto her hind legs, *changing* as she does, gold-red dingo into pretty young woman with red-gold hair, who's a twin to Lainey. Except it's not Lainey. I can tell that right away—just as I knew it was Lainey waiting for us on the shore.

This new girl—twin, clone, whatever the hell she is— smiles at us, then does a slow twirl like she's on a fashion show runway.

"Ta da!" she says.

She stands with a hand on her hip, expectant. I feel like we're supposed to applaud.

"Holy crap," Johnny manages.

His voice is tight, but at least he can say something. I'm just numb from head to foot, my tongue thick and frozen in my mouth.

"*Now* do you believe us?" she asks.

I give a slow nod. For all the impossibility of what I've just seen, I still find myself thinking that she's got the same cute accent Lainey has.

"Well, sure," Johnny says. His voice is firmer now. "Hard not to, since you pulled that trick off right in front of our eyes."

"Everything else Lainey told you is true, too."

Johnny nods. "That's as may be. But the thing I need to know right now is, did you use some kind of magic spell to make me feel so head-over-heels crazy for you? You know, because you need a couple of schmoes to help you out."

Both girls look genuinely shocked at his question. To be honest, it had never occurred to me, but as soon as it's floating there in the air between us, I have to wonder, too.

Yeah, I'd felt this immediate connection to Lainey, and— according to her—she'd felt the same thing. But what if it *was* just some kind of spell? I mean, if a dingo dog can turn into a girl, then suddenly it feels like pretty much anything you might read in a fairy tale could be true.

"God, no!" Em says. "That would just be—"

"Totally wrong," Lainey finishes.

Em nods. "How could you even think we'd do that?"

"Why wouldn't I?" Johnny says. "I mean, look at you and

look at me. You're smart and pretty, living in a nice house. I'm just some lug whose old man'd sooner hit me with a belt than say anything nice."

"We don't exactly have the nicest father, either," Em says.

"You know what I mean."

Em exchanges a glance with Lainey, then smiles at Johnny.

"Well, since you're fishing for compliments . . ." she starts.

"You know it's not like that."

"You're a handsome boy," Em goes on as though he hasn't spoken, "with a genuine artistic talent and a kind heart that you hide under bluster. I think you actually are as tough as you act, only that's not *all* you are. I also think that once you give your word, you'll keep it, no matter what."

Johnny ducks his head.

"You forgot the nice butt," Lainey says.

"I think I covered that with 'handsome.'"

Lainey turns to me, a teasing smile in her eyes.

"And speaking of nice butts," she says, "were you wondering the same thing as Johnny?"

"It never occurred to me until he said it," I tell her. "I just thought I was the luckiest person in the world."

She shakes her head. "No, that would be me."

I feel the way Johnny must have. I want to duck my head, but instead I hold that dark brown gaze of hers.

"You're making me feel dizzy," she says in a soft voice.

The whole world dissolves, and for a long moment it's as though there are only the two of us, standing here on the lake's shore. I'm about to step closer and kiss her, except then Em speaks.

"He's going to be here any moment—our father, I mean."

"And we just tell him that we're . . . betrothed," Johnny says, "and that's it? He goes away and you're free?"

"If only. No, that'll just stop him from taking us. We'll still have to face Dingo, and that'll be a whole different story."

"What will he do?" I ask.

Em shakes her head. "We really don't know. All we do know is that together we'll be strong. Whether we'll be strong enough to stand up to him . . ."

Her voice trails off. For a long moment silence hangs between us. Lainey reaches for my hand, and I give her fingers a squeeze. Em and Johnny are studying each other. I think they're about to kiss, but then Lainey's fingers tighten on mine and Em lifts her head as though she's sniffing the air.

"He's here," Em says.

I can't hear anything, but she turns to look north along the beach. Then we all hear the crunch of footsteps on the stones and see a tall figure approaching us. He's dressed in dark clothing, and it's too far away to make much of his features, but the moonlight catches his hair, which is the same red-gold as Lainey's and Em's.

Johnny shifts his position. He stands with the barrel of his rifle pointed at the ground, hidden by the length of his leg from the newcomer's view.

There's no doubt in my mind that this is Tallyman, and any jokes I had in my head earlier about that old Belafonte song are gone. This isn't somebody who's going to be tallying bananas to a Calypso beat. This guy exudes a menacing presence—a dark and dangerous vibe that makes Johnny's dad seem almost benign.

Oddly—considering his dingo blood—he moves more like a cat than a canine, sleek and graceful as he makes his way toward us. When he gets closer, we can see his features. He smiles, but there's nothing warm in that smile.

"Now everything makes sense," he says. "There's two of you pups, not just the one."

"Rack off," Em says. "Just leave us alone."

"Now, daughter. Is that any way to talk to your father?"

"You're not our father."

"Biologically, you know that's not true. It's something

you'll never get away from. I'll always be your father, and you will do as I say."

Em shakes her head.

His lips form that cold smile again. "You have spirit, and I admire that, but you don't get a choice. You will come with me now."

When he says those last few words, something changes in his voice, and I feel a strange buzz in my ears. I almost want to take a step toward him. I know Lainey feels it, too—probably stronger than I do—because her fingers tighten on mine again.

I see a flash of frustration cross Tallyman's features. He takes a step toward us, but stops when Johnny raises up the muzzle of his rifle.

"We're betrothed," Em says.

Her father nods. "I see."

"So you can't force us to do anything. We're protected from you."

"From me, yes. But you still have Warrigal to deal with."

And then he vanishes.

I mean, *literally*. One moment he's standing on the beach with us, all threatening and dangerous, and the next he's just gone.

I exchange glances with Johnny. My legs feel kind of rubbery, or maybe it's that the beach feels spongy under my feet. I find I have to remember to breathe.

"Okay," I say after a moment. "That was . . . weird."

Johnny smiles. "Yeah, like a dog changing into Em wasn't."

Em punches him in the arm. "Like a what?"

"I meant dingo," he says.

"That's better."

"But it's still weird."

"It's just different," she says.

"I guess."

"So, your father," I say. "He was . . . what? Trying to hypnotize you? Because I could feel something when he was . . . you know. Wanting you to go with him."

Em nods. "I learned about it in one of Stephen's books. Among the cousins, there's a direct connection between parents and their children that gives them a certain control over us. It has to do with simple preservation of the species. It would be hard to stay hidden if your kid can just switch back and forth between human and animal shapes. But when we move out with our mate—or have made the promise to do so—it breaks the connection."

"Even though the promise isn't real?" Johnny asks.

"Cousins don't lie," Lainey says. "If we give our word, we keep it. So if we say something, no one would ever question it."

"You *never* lie?"

She shakes her head.

"Wow." Then he pauses for a moment, thinking over what it means. "So as far as you're concerned," he says, looking at Em, "we're, like, on our way to being husband and wife?"

She smiles. "Do you hate the idea?"

"No. It's just . . ."

We're all way too young to be thinking about forever, I finish in my head when his voice just trails off.

"Oh, don't worry," Em tells him. "You're human, so we won't hold you to it."

I look at Lainey, and for a moment I don't want that to be true. I *do* want to be held to it. We're not too young to make that commitment. Who says we are? Society, that's all, and society's got such a good track record of being right. All you have to do is think about how it fought against the civil rights movement, and women's liberation. And how now, when the battles are won, it tries to start the same ones all over again.

But then I think, I'm still in high school. Lainey's not even human. And I get confused all over again.

"Are you okay?" Lainey asks me.

"Yeah. Sure. There're just a lot of new things to take in."

She takes my hand, and once again doubts flee. I so don't know where all of this is going. But I do know I love her.

"What happens now?" Johnny says.

We all look to Em, but she shakes her head.

"I don't know," she says. "I guess we still have to deal with Dingo."

"He's like the head honcho of the dingoes?" Johnny asks.

She nods.

"And he knows that there are two of you now?" I ask.

She nods again. "He'd be able to sense it. But if he didn't, Tallyman would tell him."

"What's Dingo going to do?" I ask.

"I don't know. But it's going to be bad. I . . ." She looks at Lainey, then back at me. "I didn't really think a lot past dealing with Tallyman. I guess I screwed up."

Lainey shakes her head. "We had to stop living the way we were."

"But what do we do now?" Em says.

"Couldn't we talk to your stepdad?" I say. "With these reference books he's got, maybe he can come up with something to help that you couldn't."

"We can't talk to him about it. As soon as he finds out

what's happened, he's just going to pack us all up and move us away again."

There's a little lurch in my chest when she says that.

"Then maybe we could talk to my dad," I say. "He's pretty cool and knows a lot more than just trivia about records and comics."

"Yeah," Johnny says. "And wouldn't he be happy to see my face at your house."

"He's not unreasonable," I say. "He only threw you out of the store because you were being an asshole."

He bristles, and I suddenly remember the rifle he's holding. But then he shrugs and the tension leaves the air.

"You're right," he says. "I still don't think your old man'll be too thrilled to see me, but it's not like mine'd be of any use. You really think he could help?"

"I don't know. But he's been around."

"There's a big difference riding with a bike gang and what we've got happening here."

"What do you think?" I ask the twins.

"The fewer people who know about us," Em says, "the better it'll be."

Lainey nods. "But we need to get off this beach. I can feel something bad coming, and we're too exposed here."

For a long moment no one says anything. Then Johnny

clears his throat. "We can't go to any of our houses," he says, "and I'm guessing we can't go anyplace public like a diner or the pool hall."

He looks at the twins, who nod in agreement.

"That only leaves the lighthouse."

No one says anything again. There's only the sound of the wind, pushing the waves onto the shore.

"We've been up there," Em says.

Lainey nods. "And it's all boarded up."

"I can get us in," Johnny says.

Why am I not surprised?

I don't like the idea of breaking in. The old lighthouse is a historical landmark. For years there's been talk of doing something touristy with it, but no one's stepped forward to actually take on the task. I find it kind of disappointing that Johnny and his friends have probably been partying in there. At least we have a good excuse for breaking in. If Lainey says she feels something bad's coming—and considering how the twins can turn into dingoes, and the weird vibe I got off their father—I don't want to be out here on the beach to meet whatever it is. Who knows what it might be? All the monsters and demons I've seen in too many of Dad's comic books are clamoring at the back of my head, saying, "Here I come."

Once we've climbed up the rocky path to where the tall stone building stands towering above us, Johnny uses the blade of a pen knife to jimmy open the door.

"After you, ladies," he says, waving his hand with a flourish.

Em starts forward, Lainey right behind her, but Lainey pauses in the doorway.

"Wait a minute," she says. "Something's wrong. I can feel—"

She doesn't get to finish. Suddenly, there are hands on my back, pushing me into her. She, in turn, bangs into Em, and the three of us fall down in what feels like a big pile of kindling. The sticks are brittle and break under us as I land half on Lainey, half on the mess of branches.

"What the fu—" I hear Johnny say, then he grunts.

I guess someone pushed him in after us, because as I'm trying to stand, Johnny lands on me, and all the breath gets banged out of my chest.

I push him off me and manage to sit up, trying to get my bearings. I can see the night sky through the door, but it doesn't look quite right. And neither does the door. Instead of a rectangle, it's the shape of an elongated teardrop. Through it I can see a sky that's way too big, with way too many stars.

I hear Johnny curse again.

I don't hear the twins at all.

"Lainey?" I say. "Em?"

"We're right here," Lainey says.

I feel her fingers brush my chest, then trail down my arm until she can hold my hand.

"Where the hell are we?" Johnny says.

I hear him stand up, sticks crunching underfoot, and then he's blocking the odd-shaped doorway.

"Holy crap," he says in a quiet voice.

"What is it?" I ask.

"The Point's gone, man. There's just . . . you've got to see this."

I get to my feet and pull Lainey up beside me. Em crunches across the sticks until she's standing beside Johnny.

"It's the dreamworld," she says. "Our bloody father pushed us all into the dreamworld."

"The dreamworld," Johnny repeats, his voice soft.

I know what he's thinking. We've both had too much experience with dreams lately.

I feel Lainey stiffen beside me.

"What is it?" I ask her.

"I thought these were sticks underfoot," she says.

I look down. Now that my eyesight's adjusted to the dimness in here, I can see that the sticks are all white and smooth, like they've had their bark stripped off.

Lainey she lets go of my hand and stoops. When she straightens, she's holding a skull in her hand. "We have to get out of here," she says. "And try not to break any more of the bones on the way out."

"Bones?" Johnny and I say at the same time.

"Oh, Christ," he immediately adds. "She's right. What the hell *is* this place?"

"We're inside an old baobab tree," Lainey says. "That's where the guests keep the bones and spirits of their ancestors." "What do you mean, guests?" I say.

"They were the first ones to come to this land after the cousins," Lainey explains. "People call them aboriginals now, but we've always called them guests, because, right from the first, they treated us and our homeland with respect."

"Unlike the Europeans," Em says.

Johnny shakes his head. "Hey, don't look at us. We're Americans."

"And where did the first Americans come from?"

"Whatever."

"We need to get out of here," Lainey repeats. "Now."

Johnny and Em are right by the opening, so they manage to squeeze out without any more bones snapping under their feet. It's harder for Lainey and me. We have to shuffle our way through the bones, moving carefully with every step. But finally we're outside. Lainey turns back to the opening and carefully places the skull back inside. Em comes to her side, and the two of them kneel there, chanting softly. It's either just sounds, or maybe some other language, because I can't make out a word of what they're saying.

"What was that all about?" Johnny asks when they're done.

They stand up, wiping dirt from their knees.

"We were just telling the spirits that we were sorry to have intruded on their privacy," Em says.

"And what did they say?" Johnny asks.

I can't tell if he's serious, or making a joke. Em chooses to take him seriously.

"Nothing that we could hear."

There's a faint glow on the far eastern horizon. We stand there by the tree and watch the sun rise. As the light grows, I see we're on a flat plain that spreads in all directions for as far as the eye can see. The ground's just dirt and brittle scrub grass, so dead it's almost white, some half-dead brush that's barely ankle-high, and here and there, dotting the plain, a solitary tree.

The sight of them makes me turn to look at the tree we crawled out of. The bark is a smooth, grayish brown, and its branches rise up about fifty feet, growing in a tangle that looks like a bad haircut. But it's the trunk that makes my jaw drop. It has to be thirty, maybe forty, feet across, and looks like a squat, misshapen clay pot made by a novice potter. The crack we came through is a dark split that cuts down the middle.

"What did you call it again?" I ask Lainey.

"A baobab. There are thousands of them growing in the back of Bourke."

"The what?"

"The outback."

"And they're all as big as this?"

She smiles and shakes her head. "No, some of them are bigger."

"Wow."

"Lainey and I should scout around a bit," Em says.

Lainey nods. "If we're lucky, we can find a cousin or one of the guests. Every place here has a story, and they'd know them all. Once we have some idea where we are, we can figure out what to do next."

"Are we in Australia or the dreamlands?" I ask.

Em lifts her head, her nostrils quivering as though she's reading the wind.

"The dreamlands," she says. "But it's the part most directly connected to Oz."

Johnny looks from one to the other of the twins. "I thought Miguel and I were supposed to be protecting you. How can we do that if you take off on your own?"

Em smiles. "You had your turn on the beach. Now it's ours."

"I think we should stick together," I say.

Em shakes her head. "The inhabitants of this place will either be cousins or guests. Or spirits. Most of them won't talk to us if you're with us."

"She's right," Lainey adds. "Don't worry. We'll be careful."

With that, the two change into dingoes and go loping off across the plain.

"I'm never going to get used to that," I say.

I watch as they recede into the distance. They shimmer like a mirage, then suddenly I can't see them anymore.

Johnny shrugs. "I just wonder what happens to their clothes."

"Their clothes?"

He looks at me like I'm an idiot. "C'mon. One minute they're girls, the next they're a pair of dogs. So what happens to their clothes? And how come they're not nude when they change back into girls?"

"You'd like that, wouldn't you?" I say.

"You're saying you wouldn't?"

I suppose I would, but I'm not about to admit it to him. I keep slipping into this weird feeling that we could be friends, but I'm not sure I'm ready, or even interested.

121

Whenever I look at him, I see Johnny Ward, the bully. I remember all the crappy things he's done. It's hard to separate the creep I've known for years from this new, friendlier version.

"We should have brought some water," he says.

I nod. I'm thirsty, too.

"This Dingo guy," I say. "When you were dreaming about him, was he a face in a tree?"

Johnny nods.

"And he promised you could have whatever you wanted, if you just brought Em to him?"

"Pretty much. Talked tough, too, but I knew that whether it went easy or hard, he couldn't deliver."

"Why not?"

"The only thing I'd want would be Em."

There were a lot of things I didn't get about Johnny Ward, but his feelings for Lainey's sister wasn't one of them, because I knew just how he felt.

I'm creeped out being this close to what's basically a mortuary, but once the sun rises, it gets hot quickly, and the baobab's the only shade around. While I'd expect I'd be too wound up to do so, the heat and the sleepless night soon have me dozing. But I do keep jerking awake. Johnny doesn't have that problem. When I look over at him, I see he's already fast asleep.

I doze off again, twitch awake. I think I hear something this time. The sound of the wind, I guess. Except there's no wind. The dead grass and brush is absolutely still. There's nothing moving. No birds in the air. No clouds in the sky. No dingo girls, loping back to the baobab in their furry dingo shapes.

But this sound . . .

It's almost like whispering.

I look closer at Johnny. Maybe he's mumbling in his sleep.

He's not.

Then I realize the sound's coming from the opening in the baobab, that narrow slit in the enormous trunk of the tree that spit us out into this desolate landscape.

You're only imagining it, I tell myself, and maybe I am. It could just be my guilt, because that's the weird thing. The owners of those bones are long dead and gone, but I still feel guilty for the way we were tromping all over them.

There are so many other things you'd think I'd be obsessing about. The fact that we're *here*, wherever the heck here *is*. Or that my new girlfriend's a were-dingo. That her father can just appear and disappear. That there's some weird face in a tree that talks to me in my dreams.

These are all seriously bizarre things to suddenly have in your life. But, no. All I can think about are the bones hidden away in the hollow of the baobab.

Finally, I can't take it anymore, and I get up and walk over to the opening. I glance at Johnny—still sleeping—then stick my head into the darkness.

There's nothing. No sound. No whispers. Just the light coming in from over my shoulders, illuminating a horrific bed of human bones. Leg bones, arm bones. Skulls and vertebrae.

I don't know what I was expecting. The bones to be sitting up, animated like in that Johnny Depp pirate movie. Or maybe ghosts.

But it's just a strange mortuary. A hollow tree in the middle of nowhere. Back of Bourke, as Lainey put it, whatever or wherever Bourke is.

I pull my head out for a moment, blinking at the bright light before I can check to see if Johnny's still sleeping. Then I stick my head back in, my chest leaning against the narrow V at the bottom of the opening.

"Look," I say, feeling stupid, but compelled, nevertheless, to say something. "Like the girls said, we're really sorry about walking all over you the way we did. We'd no idea you were there. I know ignorance isn't really an excuse, so . . . I just want to say I'm sorry. And . . . you know . . . if there's anything I can do to . . . I don't know . . . make it up to you . . ."

My voice trails off. This is so stupid.

But then I hear a whisper again. Not in the air, but in my head.

Anything?

I scrape my ear against the side of the opening as I scrabble backward. I look around, but there's no one here. No talking turkey, no face in the wood. Johnny's still asleep.

Why does everybody in the dreamlands have to talk inside your head? It's unbelievably creepy, like they're actually right there with you, inside your skull.

Well, boy? the voice asks.

Slowly, I return to the opening and poke my head back in.

"Who . . . who's talking?" I ask.

Who do you think?

"Man, I just don't know anymore."

There's a dry chuckle in my head.

Once I was a man, the voice says. *A blackfella, treated with less respect than a horse or a cattle dog. Now all that's left of me are bones and a dwindling spirit, cut off from my homeland.*

"You . . . all those bones are yours?"

Again the chuckle. *Hardly. But I speak for them. I speak for us all.*

I give my sore ear a rub and take a steadying breath. "What do you want me to do?" I ask.

Nothing hard. Just bury this—

There's suddenly something small and hard in my free hand. A bone, I realize. A small bone from a toe or a finger.

—in sacred ground.

That seems like a reasonable request, but I'm not feeling as trusting as I might have felt a week or so ago. Once everything changes, it's hard to know what's real anymore. What's right and what's wrong.

No, scratch that. I haven't lost my moral compass. But I'm no longer one hundred percent sure I can tell who are the good guys, and who aren't.

"Will anybody be hurt if I do this?" I ask.

No. We will be healed. Connected again to the world we left behind.

"Did someone do this to you—you know, stick all your bones inside this tree?"

I don't know. We slept, as even spirits do. When we woke, we were here, in this dreamland. I . . . I think we became forgotten by our descendants, and so were cut loose from the world.

I'm not going to pretend I really understand what I'm being told, but this doesn't seem to be too big a deal. Bury a little bone in sacred ground. But then it occurs to me . . .

"When you say 'sacred ground,'" I ask, "does that mean I have to go to Australia to do it?"

No, any sacred place will do. All the world is connected. Everyone knows that. The bird in the air, the roo in the bush, the mozzie in the swamp. Only you white fellas forget that.

"Um, right. And how will I know if the ground's sacred?"

You've a lot of questions, boy.

"That's because there's a lot I don't know."

I feel a smile in my head. *If you understand that much, perhaps there's hope for you yet. You will know sacred ground when you stand on it. Open yourself up and let the spirits of your ancestors guide you.*

My fingers are closed around the little bone. It's cold against my skin, though my body heat should have warmed it up by now.

"I can do that," I tell the invisible presence inside the baobab. "I can try."

Then your apology is accepted.

And oddly enough, my heart feels lighter at those words.

"I won't let you down," I say.

"Who are you talking to?" Johnny says.

His voice startles me, but I pull my head out of the opening without banging my ear again. I turn to see him sitting up, still sleepy-eyed from his nap.

"Nobody," I say.

"You're not going flaky on me, are you?"

I shake my head. Moving casually, I stick my hand in my pocket and let the little bone rest in the bottom. I can feel its cold presence against my thigh.

"How long was I asleep?" he asks.

"Not long. A couple of hours, maybe. Did you dream at all?"

"Not so's I remember." He gets up and stretches, then looks around. "Have the girls been back?"

"No, and it's been hours now."

Johnny lifts his head then, his gaze caught by something behind me. When I turn, it's like we summoned them with our conversation, because here they come running toward us through the scrub, two tawny dingoes. I expect them to stop and change back before they get to us, but the most enthusiastic of the two charges right for me and jumps up, paws against my chest. I push her down and kneel so our heads are more at the same level.

I put my hands on either side of her face and ruffle the

fur under her ears, and then the strangest thing happens. I've seen the change—twice now—but I've never felt it. I feel the fur recede under my hands, become skin, the shape of her bones and muscles changing until it's Lainey facing me, my palms on the soft skin of her neck under her ears, her red-gold hair spilling over my hands. She leans closer and gives me a kiss.

"I was worried about you," I say.

"And I was worried about you."

"Me? I wasn't the one who went off exploring."

"No," she says. "You were the one who stayed behind, right where Tallyman put us. Anything could have happened to you. We should have thought of that."

I think of the whispering ghost and the cold bone in my pocket.

"We were okay," I tell her. "Johnny had a nap, and I was talking to the ghosts inside the tree."

"Ha-ha."

She stands up and offers her hand. I think it's funny that she's going to pull me up, but she does it effortlessly. Turns out she's a lot stronger than she looks.

I glance over to see Em leaning against Johnny's chest. They have their arms around each other, and he's looking off into the distance with pretty much the goofiest expression I've ever seen on his face.

"I wish I had a camera," I say, pitching my voice low.

"Oh, come on," Lainey says. "They're cute."

"Define cute."

She punches my arm in reply. Considering how easily she pulled me to my feet, I'm guessing she held back. A lot. And I'm glad she did.

"So, what did you find out?" I ask.

Johnny and Em step apart and come over to join us.

"Nothing much," Lainey says.

Em nods. "And that's the problem. This place"—she gives a vague wave of her arm that encompasses everything—"it's like a dumping ground, and it's so far away from anything any of us might find familiar that, unless we can find a guide, it's going to take us a very long time to get home."

I don't like the sound of that.

"My dad's going to be worried," I say.

Lainey nods. "Stephen's not going to be too happy, either."

Johnny laughs, but the humor never reaches his eyes.

"My old man is never even going to know I'm gone," he says.

"What did you mean by a dumping ground?" I ask Em.

Lainey answers. "We've never seen one before. We've hardly ever been in the dreamworld before. But Stephen told us about places like this. It's just where stuff gets put that no one has a use for. This plain used to be somewhere else in the dreamworld, but it must have been in somebody's way."

"And," Em adds, "since there isn't much use for an empty place like this, it just got plucked up and dumped here in the back of nowhere."

"With everything in it," I say.

She nods. "Except there's nothing here except for these baobabs and some scrub. We haven't found a single cousin, or any kind of wildlife. Which makes sense, because this little piece of world couldn't have been moved if it was being used by anyone, or anything."

"Then what about the bones inside the tree?" I ask. "And the ancestral spirits connected to them?"

Em gives me a considering look, and I realize that, for the first time, she's seeing me more in the way her sister sees me. It's not that she's been as mean to me as she was that day on the beach, but she hasn't been particularly warm, either.

"What I want to know is," Johnny says, "what do we do?"

Em shrugs. "We can try to find the borders of this place and get to another part of the dreamworld."

"And once we get someplace else," Lainey adds, "we'll have to keep doing the same thing until we find something familiar."

Em nods. "But that's going to take forever. Tallyman knew what he was doing when he sent us here."

"Then we should get started," Johnny says. "Did you find any water out there?'

Lainey shakes her head.

"There's another option," Em says. "We can try going back through the tree. If there was a door leading here, there'll be another leading out. It probably won't take us back to Harnett's Point, but it'll be quicker than hiking across this plain."

"We can't go back into the tree," I say. "The—"

"Oh, for Christ's sake," Johnny breaks in. "Don't be such a wuss. They're only bones."

"If you'd let me finish?"

"Sure. Whatever."

"I was going to say that the spirits those bones belonged to weren't happy the first time we went stomping all over them."

"You really *were* talking to ghosts?" Lainey asks.

I nod.

"Come on," Johnny says. "Like there's any such thing as ghosts."

"Yeah," I tell him. "That's just crazy, isn't it? Not like were-dingoes and stepping through the door of a lighthouse and ending up here."

"Were-dingoes?" Em says.

I ignore her, my gaze fixed on Johnny.

"Okay," he says. "Point fricking taken."

"Were-dingoes?" Em repeats.

"I think it's kind of cute," Lainey says. "You know." She puts on a spooky voice. "I was a teenage were-dingo."

A smile twitches in the corner of Em's mouth.

"But why did your father send us here?" I ask. "He must have had something planned."

Lainey shrugs. "I guess he just wanted to put us on hold until he can figure out a way to bring us to Dingo."

"I thought you had to go willingly to him."

"That's true," she says. "But it also works if someone willingly gives us to him. That's what those dreams were all about."

"Jesus," Johnny says. "Are you just supposed to be property?"

"I know. It's twisted. Especially when, normally, cousins aren't even into owning things."

"Why do you think Tallyman would do it?" I ask. "I can't believe anybody would have a kid just so that they can trade her in for favors."

"Do you really want to stick around to find out?" Em asks.

I shake my head.

133

"Then we need to go back the way we came—and don't worry," she adds before I can protest again. "We'll be careful where we step."

Lainey nods. She leads the way to the slit in the tree and is the first to go through. I'm right behind her and hear her speak, her voice echoing in the hollow space.

"Spirits," she says. "We mean no disrespect. We will be as careful as possible."

You may pass, that ghost voice says in my head. *Your companion has already earned you a safe passage.*

I have my hand on Lainey's shoulder as I step carefully inside the baobab so I can keep my balance. I feel her shiver as the words resound in her head.

"Holy crap," I hear Johnny say behind me.

I guess everybody can hear it this time.

Lainey takes my hand when I'm standing beside her. I find that by shuffling my feet, I can push through the bones without breaking any.

"What did you promise them?" she asks.

"I'm just doing them a favor," I say. "They need help getting connected back to the world again."

"Miguel," she starts.

"Don't worry. I made sure nobody would be hurt if I did what they asked. It's all cool."

"But *what* did you promise you'd do?"

"I'll tell you later."

We make room for Johnny and Em. I hear a bone crack under one of their shoes—probably Johnny's, I think. I feel a swell of anger in my head. It's the ghost's, not mine, but it feels like mine. I make an effort to keep my voice level.

"Tell them you're sorry," I say.

"Are you serious, man?"

"Just do it."

I hear a soft thump—Em elbowing him, I'm guessing.

"Okay, already," Johnny says. "I'm sorry."

"How does this work now?" I ask Lainey.

It's Em who responds.

"Anyplace that's in between is a place of power," she says. "The moment between day and night. The place between the water and the shore. And doorways. Especially doorways."

I give a slow nod. I always feel as though the world's full of all kinds of promise and potential at dawn, or at dusk.

"That makes sense," I say. "As much as anything has in the past day or so."

Lainey squeezes my hand.

"So, what we need to do," Em goes on, "is keep our backs to the opening behind us. We'll keep our eyes closed, too, and focus on the beach where we first met. Then we turn, and, with our eyes still closed, we step back out the opening."

"And that works?" Johnny asks.

Em hesitates, then says, "Well, it's supposed to. And it's supposed to be easier when you're doing it on this side of the boundary between the worlds. But it's not something I've ever tried on my own. The few times we've crossed over it was always Stephen who took us."

"So, no guarantees," Johnny says.

"No. And we could end up farther away from where we want to be, rather than closer."

No one says anything for a long moment.

"Screw it," Johnny says. "I never planned to live forever. Let's do it."

Lainey gives my hand another squeeze—I don't know if it's to comfort me, or herself. It doesn't matter. I squeeze her hand back and close my eyes.

Focus on the beach, I think. That's easier said than done. But then Em's voice comes to me from the darkness.

"Call up the smells of fish and weeds," she says. "The soft sound of the waves on the shore. The faint whisper of the wind in the weeds at the top of the ridge. Feel the pebbles shift underfoot."

That helps. A lot, actually. As I focus on her voice, I can actually start to hear the water and the wind. I can smell that faint undercurrent of decaying weeds and fish that you get anywhere in the Point where they don't regularly clean the beaches.

"Keep your eyes closed," Em says, "and turn around."

We do so, careful of where we're stepping. The light coming in through the slit of the baobab's trunk is bright on my closed eyelids.

"Everybody take each other's hand."

I'm already holding Lainey's. I reach out in the dark until my fingers meet Johnny's hand. We grab hold of each other, and I wonder for a moment how he's holding his rifle. But then the butt of the rifle bangs against my knee, and I realize it's hanging by its strap from his shoulder.

"Follow me now," Em says. "And keep your eyes closed."

Good-bye, I think to the ghost inside the tree. Then we're moving forward, back through the slit, out onto the plain. Except . . .

"I can so *feel* the beach," Em says. "Can't you?"

She's good at this. Even though I'm stepping out onto the sun-drenched plain, the bright light on my eyelids is fading to dark. The solid ground of the plain gives away to the shift of pebbles underfoot. I almost open my eyes, but Lainey's still inside the tree. So I wait for her to join us.

But somewhere between her passage out of the tree to join the rest of us on the beach and her standing beside me,

I feel everything change. The smell of the lakeshore is gone, replaced by that of an old forest—deep and musty. The wind stills, and the sound of the lake disappears. I feel a leaf brush my face, rough on my cheek.

"Oh no," I hear Em say.

Then I open my eyes and I understand her dismay.

We're in Dingo's forest. Not only that, we're in among the branches that have rooted around his giant tree. And there he is, the face in the wood, looking out at us, smiling.

You're sooner than I expected, he says.

I'm too stunned to do anything but stare. The girls are silent, too. But Johnny swings his rifle from his shoulder. The sound of him drawing the bolt back to jack a bullet into the firing chamber is loud. It makes me jump. The muzzle of his rifle lifts until it's pointing right at the face staring at us out of the bark.

You can't kill a tree with a bullet, I think.

But Johnny doesn't even get the chance to try.

You ever watch one of those movies where rocks come to life, or trees start to move? I mean, move without the benefit of wind. It doesn't matter how good the special effects are. When I see something like that, all I can think is, Oh, *please.* It's just so stupid.

But it's not stupid. It's scary as hell when a branch of Dingo's giant tree whips down from the canopy, sinuous and as animated as a snake, and tugs the rifle out of Johnny's hands.

Johnny makes a grab for it, but more branches come down, winding around him until he can't move. I take a step in his direction, but all that does is focus the tree's attention on me. More branches come to life, wrapping around me and pinning my arms to my side.

They feel horrible. Soft and hard at the same time. Fleshy, but with a rough bark.

We don't need you here anymore, Warrigal says. *I don't think the girls have any more use for you. I know that I don't.*

Lainey reaches for me, trying to get a grip on the branches that are wound around me, but she can't help. She can't stop Dingo. None of us can. I feel myself lifted. It's like my chest's being crushed as the weight of my body hangs from the branches. Johnny's in the air, too. We dangle there for a moment, then the branches fling us away.

Johnny starts to yell, "I'll kill you, you motherfu—"

But everything goes black, and when we land, it's on the beach on Harnett's Point.

"—cker," Johnny finishes just as we hit the ground.

We sprawl in the stones, skidding a few feet. Johnny's immediately on his feet, fists cocked, turning in a slow circle. But there's no threat here. I lie on the pebbles for a moment, nursing my bruises and trying to catch my breath. The cloud cover completely broke while we were away. Staring up, I see that the sky is rich with stars, the moon hanging over the Point.

I sit up, then slowly get to my feet. Was any of it real? I find myself thinking.

I have this big ache in my chest—the hole that losing Lainey's left there. But it feels old, like it happened a long time ago. In another life.

Or in a dream . . .

Johnny starts to walk away, pausing only when I call after him. He turns to look at me.

"What?" he asks.

"We have to do something," I say. "The girls—"

"You heard what the dude in the tree said. They don't have any more use for us."

"Yeah, but *they* didn't say it. Whatever he wants them for, it'll only work if they go willingly, and they didn't do that."

"If they go willingly," he repeats. "Or if someone willingly gives them up."

"Which *we* didn't do."

He nods. "So what does that tell you?"

"I don't know what you're getting at," I say.

"If you didn't bring us to the freak face in the tree—and

I know I sure as hell didn't—then it had to be them. Or one of them. We were played."

"*Played.* Played how? They were trying to stay away from Dingo."

"That's what they said."

"That makes no sense at all."

He shakes his head. "Look, it's done, okay? I don't know what the hell happened tonight, but it's done. And you want to know what I think? I think they were just using us all along."

"For what? Ten minutes ago you were holding on to Em and looking all moony-faced, so don't—"

"Grow up," he tells me. "You're looking at the world like it's fair. But that's not the way things work. And you know what? Maybe we got suckered, maybe we didn't, but we're out of the picture now, so it doesn't much matter."

"You're everything I always thought you were," I tell him, "and nothing like whatever the hell it was Em saw in you."

"You don't know jack about what I am," he says.

"I know you're a coward and a bully."

He closes the distance between us. Before I realize what he's going to do, he hits me hard in the stomach. I buckle over as all the air goes out of me. He pushes me while I'm off balance, and I fall on the pebbles again.

"Maybe once upon a time your old man was some tough biker," he says, "but you're nothing, Schreiber. So stay out of my way, or you're really going to get hurt."

Then he walks away again. I lie there on the beach, holding my stomach. This time I don't try to call him back. I close my eyes, but all I see is Lainey. So I get back on my feet.

I'm not giving up on her.

I haven't the first clue how to get back to that giant tree. Maybe it's impossible. But I know one place that I can go ask.

We were gone for the better part of a day, but it seems like only an hour or so has passed here in the Point. I take the path up to the lighthouse because I'm feeling too sore to go scrabbling up the rocks behind the B and B that Lainey's stepfather bought. The door to the lighthouse is still ajar, and I stick my head in to see if whatever magic sent us to the plain is still working. I can't feel anything, but what do I know about magic?

I toss a pebble in and hear it go rattling across the stone floor until it finally settles somewhere in the dark. I have another weak moment when I'm questioning if it ever really happened. Em and Lainey turning into dingoes, the passage to another world. Or maybe what I'm having is a rational moment. But then I put my hand in my pocket. The little bone's still there, and it's still unnaturally cold.

No, it happened.

And that means Lainey and Em really do need my help.

But will their stepfather even listen to me?

There's only one way to find out.

I make my way down from the lighthouse to the street and start for the B and B. I keep to the shadows; I'm not really sure why, but I'm glad I did because I haven't taken more than a few steps when I see a big tawny dog at the far end of the block, walking down the middle of the street.

No, not a dog. A dingo. Tallyman.

I freeze in the shadows, afraid he's seen me, but all his attention is focused on the same place I was heading.

What's Tallyman doing here?

Then I remember my conversation with Johnny. The girls have to go willingly to Dingo in his tree. No matter what Johnny says, I know they didn't suddenly just give up and agree. But what if their stepfather was being threatened? I know they care about Stephen. So if Tallyman was to grab him . . .

This I can't deal with on my own.

I wait until Tallyman darts into the front yard of the B and B, then I pull out my cell phone and call Dad.

I have a good relationship with my dad. I'm not saying

he'd approve of everything I've ever done, but he trusts me and respects me, which is more than I can say for some other kids' fathers. Like Johnny's . . .

Don't go there, I tell myself. Don't start feeling sorry for the prick.

Anyway the point is, I can ask my dad to help and not to ask questions, and he'll do both. He won't hold off with the questions forever—but I don't need forever. I just need long enough to sort this out. And by that point he might have seen enough of this comic book world I've fallen into to know it's all real, so I won't have to deal with his disbelief.

He picks up on the second ring.

"Dad," I say, without any preamble, "I need your help, and I need it fast."

"Jesus, Miguel, what's—"

"There's no time, Dad. I just need you to come here. And try not to make any noise."

I tell him where I am. I know he's got a hundred questions, but all he says is, "I'll be right there."

We live only a couple of blocks away, but he must have run the whole way, because in less than five minutes I see my dad jogging up the block toward me, his footsteps barely audible on the pavement. I'd already moved to another part of the street after I called, hiding in a new set of shadows so that I could intercept him before he inadvertently let Tallyman know we're here. I guess he's still in pretty good shape, because he's not even out of breath when he comes abreast of the hedge that I'm crouched beside.

"Dad!" I say in a loud whisper.

"Mig—" he starts, but I cut him off with a finger to my lips.

"I'll explain everything later," I tell him, still whispering. "But right now we need to keep that dog out of Lainey's house."

I point to the B and B and his gaze follows my finger. I've been watching Tallyman ever since I called Dad. He's been circling the house in his dingo shape, looking for a way in. When I point him out to Dad now, he's up on his hind legs, peering into yet another window.

Dad makes the connection immediately.

"Is that the dog that was hanging around our house?" he asks.

"Yeah, except it's not a dog, it's a dingo."

"A dingo."

"They're sort of Australia's version of a wolf or a coyote."

But Dad's not interested in zoology right now.

"Listen, son," he says. "You need to tell me—"

I cut him off again with a shake of my head.

"There's no time to explain it properly right now," I say. "And you probably won't believe me when I do try. But until we do something about that dog, Lainey and her sister are in all kinds of trouble."

But it turns out that I don't need to explain, or try to make Dad believe anything. As we watch, Tallyman comes around to the front door of the B and B. He stands there as a dingo for a long moment, and then he shifts into his man shape.

"I . . . I didn't see that," Dad says in strained voice.

"No, you totally did."

I look at him and he's shaking his head.

"This is real, Dad," I tell him.

Up by the B and B, Tallyman has worked a large stone free from a low stone wall that runs along the flower bed. I tug Dad's sleeve and point.

"We can't let him get in," I say.

He nods.

Johnny Ward was so full of it, I think. My dad *might* have been a tough guy? No, he *is* one. Because without even stopping to think about it, he shakes off his surprise and trots across the street, pulling a tire iron out from where it had been stashed under his jean jacket.

I hurry after him.

We're quiet as we come up off the street, but Tallyman hears us all the same. His eyes widen slightly when he recognizes me, but then he's lobbing a great chunk of stone at us as effortlessly as if it's a basketball.

I keep forgetting how strong these cousins are.

Dad and I take off in opposite directions, and the stone crashes onto the street behind us. There's no time for Tallyman to get another, so he charges Dad. I don't think he saw the tire iron, but he sure feels it when Dad brings it up and whacks him on the side of the head. I hear the dull thud of the impact, and my stomach does a little flip at the horrible sound—then he goes down like a rag doll, all his limbs boneless and splaying.

Dad gets to him just in time to keep him from smashing his head on the pavement. He lowers him the rest of the way to the ground, then steps back again, the tire iron ready.

"Oh, jeez," I say. "He's not dead, is he?"

"I hope not. I didn't put my full weight behind the blow. You don't have to with a tire iron—not if you want the other guy to live." He reaches into his pocket—looking for his cell phone, I guess, because he adds, "We need to call the police."

"Not yet, Dad," I say.

A puzzled look flashes on his face. Before he can follow it up with a question, I march up to the front door of the B and B and hammer on it with my fist.

"You might try the bell," Dad says.

But I don't need to. The door opens inward with a jerk, and there's a man standing there. I'm guessing he was already on his way to the door, drawn by the sound of the stone Tallyman threw—the crash of it hitting the pavement.

"Stephen?" I ask.

From the bits and pieces that Lainey had told me, I was expecting somebody very different. I thought he'd be scholarly. In my head I had a picture of a thin man, bookish, with glasses. Instead, he looks like the surfer dude Chris wishes he was—shaggy blond hair, handsome, tanned. He's wearing a T-shirt over a pair of baggy, three-quarter-length cargo pants, and he's barefoot.

He looks from Dad to me, then gives a slow nod in response to my question.

"Do you have any idea what time it is?" he says.

Before either Dad or I can respond, his gaze drops to where Tallyman sprawls on the walk by our feet. When his gaze rises again, there's a dark light in his eyes.

"Who are you people?" he says.

His voice is mild, but there's a crackle of power in it. He seems to stand taller, filling the doorway now. I remember

Lainey telling me that he can't shift shapes, but she also told me that he set some kind of magical protection around Em and her. Magic's something I don't think Dad can fend off with a tire iron.

Dad picks up on the threat right away.

"Now let's all take it easy," he says. He nods to where Tallyman lies. "This guy was trying to break into your house. We're just here to make sure you're okay."

"You and the girls," I add.

That gaze of his goes even darker.

"What girls?" he says.

Dad gives me a puzzled look, but I ignore it. Lainey's stepfather is starting to tick me off.

"Oh, I know," I say. "There's only supposed to be one, so they take turns going out of the house where you've got some kind of magic whatzit to keep them safe. But they're both gone now, and unless you want Dingo to eat them, or whatever it is he's going to do, we'd better come up with a plan to get them back."

Stephen doesn't quite give me a slack-jawed look, but I know he's taken aback.

"Miguel," Dad says from beside me.

There's a warning in his voice, but I hold Stephen's gaze.

"Let me ask you again," he says. The threat isn't gone

from his eyes, but it's been tempered with curiosity and—I guess—worry. "Who are you people?"

"I'm Miguel Schreiber," I say. "Lainey's boyfriend. And this is my dad."

"Mike," Dad says, and offers his hand.

"Stephen Howe." He shakes Dad's hand, but it's an automatic gesture. I can tell he's still trying to figure out the "Lainey's boyfriend" business, seeing as how he kept Em and her under such tight lock and key.

"You might as well come in," he says.

"What about him?" Dad asks, nodding his chin at Tallyman.

Stephen sighs. "We'd better bring him as well."

It takes a while for me to tell my story. I'm not sure who's more surprised by what I have to relate—Dad, or Lainey's stepfather. Maybe it's me, because I can't believe how well Dad's taking all of this new information about shape-changing dingoes and other worlds. I guess he had years of preparation for something like this, reading all those comic books.

We're sitting in the kitchen around a big wooden table—even Tallyman, except, unlike us, he's duct-taped to his chair. Stephen wound the tape around him in such a way that he wouldn't be able to escape even if he shifted back into a dingo, but so far he slumps in his chair and hasn't come around yet.

When I finally run out of story, I look at Stephen, then at Dad.

"You're not saying anything, Dad."

"What am I supposed to say?" he asks with a shake of his head. "I saw a dog change into a man and thought I'd stumbled into the middle of a Michael Ploog comic. After that, it's all just *Twilight Zone*, isn't it? Any damn thing can happen, and it seems like it has."

"I didn't set out to get involved in all of this," I say.

"I know, son."

But Stephen breaks in, "Then why did you get involved? Do you have any idea how hard it's been to keep the girls safe? But you just waltz in and undo everything I've worked for these past few years."

His eyes don't look so dark and scary anymore, but it's obvious he's pissed off, and I'm still nervous. But I give him the truth.

"I love her," I tell him. "I love Lainey. I got involved because she asked me to. She and Em were tired of living locked up like prisoners."

"It was for their own safety."

"They still felt like prisoners."

"You love her," he says.

I nod.

"And you've known her for, what? A week?"

"I know," I say. "It freaks me a little, too. But it doesn't change the way I feel."

"How old are you?" Stephen asks. "Fifteen? Sixteen?"

"I'm seventeen."

"The same age as my girls. How can you even know what love means? You're still children."

"Well, now," Dad says before I can speak, "the way I see it, love runs true, regardless of age."

Stephen starts to say something, but Dad rolls over him the same way Stephen did me.

"My best friend back in high school was a guy named Hector," Dad says. "Great guy—but that's not the point. The point is, Hector started dating this girl in ninth grade. He and Malena got married after graduation, and they're still happily married now, thirty-five years later. So maybe my son and your daughter could make a go of it, or maybe they wouldn't, but if they did make it work, would you really want to take a lifetime of happiness away from your girl?"

Stephen frowns at him. "I hardly need to be lectured on—"

"You know," I say, breaking in, "it doesn't matter if you

like me or not. What's important is that we get Lainey and Em back."

Stephen looks like he wants to argue some more, but then he nods.

"You're right, of course," he says.

"So *is* there anything we can do?"

"There's nothing we can do—at least not your father or me. But you . . . it took me a while, but I can see the cousin blood in you. A touch of corbae—which is good. Crows are a particularly influential and plentiful clan in these parts. But there's also a dram's drop of some kind of canid. I can't tell exactly what. Fox, maybe. Or maybe one of Cody's kin."

I give him a look like he's grown a second head.

"You're saying I can turn into a bird or a fox?" I say.

He shakes his head. "No more than I can become a dingo. The bloodline is too thin. But this might help explain Lainey's instant trust in you."

I would have felt disappointed that I couldn't shift shapes, but I'm too busy taking offense at the last thing he said.

"Or maybe we just like each other," I say.

"And it also explains," he goes on, as though I haven't spoken, "why Dingo didn't kill you outright. The bloodlines are thin, yes, but if he killed you out of hand, and someone spoke up on your behalf to one of the clan chiefs, it would still be cause for a blood feud."

Dad looks at Tallyman. "I thought *this* guy was the dingo."

"He's part of the same clan, but Warrigal is the chief of their clan, and his common name is Dingo. He claims to be the first of us, already walking the world when Sun Woman made the animals long ago, but I have my doubts. The true first dingo would have a larger spirit and use his time for more than Warrigal's endless schemes."

I *so* don't understand what he's talking about.

"Whatever," I say. "The only thing I want to know right now is if there's anything *I* can do."

Stephen looks at Dad, before he returns his attention to me, and says, "Getting you back to where Dingo is keeping the twins shouldn't be too much of a problem. There will still be some lingering traces on the beach of your passage between the worlds. If both you and Johnny return as closely as possible to the spot where you reappeared in this world, I should be able to connect you to those traces and use them to send you back."

I still have no real idea what he's talking about, but that's only the smallest part of the problem here. I think back to my last conversation with Johnny, the one that would've ended in a fistfight if I'd gotten up from where he'd pushed me.

"I don't think that we can count on Johnny," I say.

"We have to," Stephen tells me. "Everything needs to be as close as possible to how it was when you arrived. The same people, wearing the same clothes, in the same place."

I decide to let that go for the moment, because there seems to be an even bigger flaw in his logic.

"And then what?" I ask. "The last time Johnny and I were there, the tree branches just picked us up and threw us back into this world. What's to stop that from happening again?"

"You'll have to issue a challenge to Dingo, in the name of the clans whose kinship you carry in your blood. For the sake of his honor—and because of your cousin bloodlines—he'll have to deal with the challenge before he can do anything else."

"But he knows I don't have any connection to any clans or cousins or whatever."

"You didn't have any awareness of it," Stephen says, "which isn't the same thing. But now you know. You could always try calling on them and seeing if any respond."

"Yeah, right."

"But it's not really relevant. Anyone else can petition the clan chiefs on your behalf, and you can be sure I would if Dingo didn't honor the challenge."

"I don't even know how I'd *survive* a challenge."

"Yeah," Dad says, echoing my own feelings. "Miguel's a tough kid, but he's no match for a full-grown man who can also turn into some kind of wild animal."

"Except Dingo can't do anything," Stephen says. "Remember, he's trapped in a tree. And as long as Miguel doesn't agree to Dingo's naming an intermediary to take his place, Dingo will have to forfeit the challenge as soon as it's made."

I sort of understand where this is going now, but it's making me uneasy. I remember Lainey talking about honor—how among the cousins it's the most important thing in the world. More important even than their lives. So to go into this, already knowing that that Dingo's at such a disadvantage . . .

"I know Lainey and Em's lives are at stake," I say, "but this doesn't seem like a very honorable way to rescue them."

"The point is their lives *are* at stake," Stephen says. "So unless you can come up with a better plan . . . ?"

"No, I just . . ."

I look at Dad.

"I know what you're thinking," he says, "and I'm proud of you for wanting to play fair, but I don't see this as the time or place. It's not like this dingo man played fair with you or the twins."

"But that's just it," I say. "He did—in his own way. He might have tricked us, but we chose to go to his world. And while he's keeping the twins there against their will, he's not going to do anything to them until they agree to it. Which," I add, glancing at where we still have Tallyman bound to the chair, "is why he was here. He was probably supposed to kidnap Stephen so that Dingo could use him as a threat to make the twins agree."

"Which isn't playing fair," Dad repeats.

"But does that mean we should be like him?"

"If it's to save my girls," Stephen says, "then yes. Absolutely."

Dad turns to him. "I just need your assurance that Miguel isn't going to get hurt."

"I can't give you that."

"And I can't not go," I say.

"Then I'm coming with you," Dad says.

Stephen shakes his head. "It needs to be Miguel and his friend Johnny. The two of them came here and left traces of that passage. Only the two of them can go back."

"I can do this, Dad," I say. "As long as I can get Johnny to agree to come with me."

"You want me to help you with that?"

"Considering the history between the two of you?" I say.

He nods in reluctant agreement.

I stand up. "I should go talk to Johnny."

But before I can leave the room, I hear a voice in my head—an unpleasant, intrusive scrape of words.

Boy, the voice says, *no matter what you have planned, Dingo will eat you alive.*

I realize Tallyman's awake and faking unconsciousness. I wonder how long he's been conscious, how much he heard. Then I realize it doesn't matter. He isn't going anywhere.

"You'd better keep an eye on him," I say to Stephen.

Dad walks me to the front door. He hugs me.

"Be careful," he says.

"Well, yeah. Except this is just talking to Johnny."

Dad shakes his head. "Johnny Ward has a human side," he says. "Who would have thought?"

When I was telling my story, I left out the bit at the end where Johnny shoved me to the ground. I just said we disagreed and he went home. I don't know why I did that, but now I'm glad I did. If Dad knew about Johnny's current animosity toward me, he'd never let me go talk to him, never mind head back into fairyland in his company.

"Make sure Tallyman doesn't get loose," I tell Dad. "I think he's just faking unconsciousness."

I don't tell Dad that I heard Tallyman's voice in my

head. I think I've stretched his credulity enough for one night.

"Don't worry," Dad says. "He's not going anywhere."

He gives me a final hug, then I set off for Johnny's house. I'm not looking forward to this. Even if I can get past his drunken father and his slutty sister without any trouble, Johnny will still probably try to kick my head in.

Except it doesn't turn out that way.

I find Johnny sitting on the curb about a block away from his house. He's staring down at the pavement, his shoulders slouched. He doesn't even look up as I approach.

"Hey, Johnny," I say.

He doesn't respond, but he doesn't tell me to piss off, either. That's got to be a good sign, right? I wait a moment, then sit down beside him.

"How come you're sitting out here?" I ask.

"I can't go inside." He turns to look at me, then stares down at the pavement again. "That was my old man's rifle I lost in wherever the hell it was we went. When he finds out it's gone, he's gonna kill me."

"Maybe we can get it back."

"Yeah, right."

I wait a moment, then add, "I'm going back. The twins' stepfather can get us there."

"You just don't get it, do you? The twins don't want anything from us, man."

"You don't know that."

He shakes his head. "Nothing good ever happens to a Ward. And if it does, it just gets taken away."

"I'm still going. And if it's true that she doesn't care for me anymore, I want to hear it from Lainey herself. I want her to look me in the eye and tell me."

"But you don't believe it."

I shake my head.

"Yeah, well, good luck with that."

"The thing is," I tell him, "the only way Stephen can send me back is with you. We both have to go, or neither of us can. I'm not sure what the deal is. It's something to do with everything having to be the same as it was when we landed on the beach."

He turns to look at me again.

"I'm not going," he says. "I don't want to argue this with you, and I'm too tired to knock you on your ass again."

"I'm already on my ass."

"Don't push it."

"Then stop thinking only of yourself," I tell him.

"Okay," he says. "So you're back in Never-never land. Then what? In case you don't remember, we got our asses handed to us by a bunch of tree branches."

"Stephen has a plan."

I tell him what the twins' stepfather told me.

"Oh right," he says. "And Dingo's just going to let us all walk away?"

"Do you have a better idea?"

"Can't you see how this is all bullshit?"

I just look at him, then say, "Do I look stupid? Of course it sounds like bullshit. But if there's a chance Stephen's got it right, I'm taking it."

"For Lainey."

I nod.

"And you expect me to feel the same for Em," he says.

"I don't expect anything. I'm asking you for a favor."

"Because we're such good friends."

"I don't have time to argue. Will you come with me, or not? It's a chance to get your dad's rifle back."

"And get killed in the process."

"You said he was going to kill you anyway."

He doesn't say anything for the longest moment. I think he's just ignoring me, but then he laughs, without much humor.

"Well, there's that, isn't there?" he says.

He stands up and looks down at me still sitting on the curb.

"So are you coming or what?" he asks.

I nod, and we set off back to Stephen's place.

I'm surprised it was so easy to convince him, but relieved as well. I'm not saying I trust him. He could easily turn on me again. But I need him to get back into Dingo's world.

"How come you didn't take your own rifle last night?" I ask as we walk along the dark streets.

"The old man's is better."

I nod, like I know the difference, and put my hands in my pockets—until I realize that I'm subconsciously trying to emulate Johnny's nonchalant cool. As I start to take them out, the fingers of one hand touch the tiny bone at the bottom of my pocket. It's smooth against the pad of my fingertip, and still icy cold.

Just as I'd left out my scuffle with Johnny, I hadn't told Stephen or Dad about the bone. I'm not sure why. With all that's been happening, I might have forgotten I still had it for a moment, but I don't forget *why* I'm carrying it.

The eerie voice, talking to me from inside the baobab tree, is easy to call up in my memory.

Bury it in sacred ground.

The most sacred ground I know is the small graveyard behind Our Lady of Sorrows Church. One spot in particular: my mother's grave.

Dad's not a churchgoer, and neither am I. But I can remember Mom taking me to Our Lady's for mass when I was a kid, and I still come in and light a candle for her on her favorite saints' days. It's funny. I know, I was really young, but I can clearly remember this whole different way she had of looking at church. I guess it came from how she grew up in New Mexico, from the Mexican influences on Catholicism down there.

Every once in a while, I still go to Our Lady's—not just to light a candle, and for sure not for confession—but I'm always disappointed. The priest's all about God, and Jesus, and the Holy Ghost. He's neither tolerant, nor loving. It's so not like my mother's stories. Hers were all about the Virgin and the saints—that's who she spoke and prayed to. And they weren't these stern, dark-browed, distant figures. They were more like . . . I don't know. Living spirits, I guess, who are all around you and who you can actually communicate with.

When she was alive, they were real to me, too. But after they took her from me, I stopped caring about them.

The candles I lit were for my mother, not for them.

When I slipped in the back of the church during a mass, it wasn't to listen to the priest up there in his fancy robes. It was to see if I could feel my mother's presence. She seemed close only when I looked at the humble statue of Mary, off to one side of the altar, with the cross rearing high above it, majestic and—I'll admit it—a little scary.

But the Virgin's statue was a comfort, and my mother's grave even more so. If anyone could help the ghosts of the baobab tree, I knew it would be her. And since I couldn't imagine a more sacred ground, that was where the little bone needed to be buried.

I could do it when I got back from Dingo's world, but what if I didn't get back? The ghosts would be trapped inside the baobab tree forever.

"I have to make a quick detour," I tell Johnny.

Johnny doesn't come into the graveyard with me. He stands at the gate and watches as I kneel on the grass in front of my mother's gravestone, my back to him. I trail my fingers across the indented letters that shape her name.

"I miss you, Mom," I say softly.

This is the only place I ever talk to her. She's not here—no more than she's at home, or in the church when I sneak into the back aisles during mass. I know she's not. So I don't know why I talk to her here. I just do.

I take the tiny bone out of my pocket and hold its coldness in my closed fist. I remember the voice of the ghost in my head—that lingering ghost—and for the first time in a long while, I wonder if maybe she really can hear me when I talk to her.

"I know this is a stupid, dangerous thing to be doing," I say, "and I don't know why I care so much about Lainey. But I do. It's like you and Dad—I really believe that. And you'd like her, Mom.

"Anyway, I just wanted to ask you to look out for Dad if I don't make it back. I know he looks busy, with his life full of people, but they're all acquaintances, you know? Not real friends. He could sure use a friend his own age. I . . ."

My voice trails off. I can feel Johnny's presence behind me, and what am I really doing anyway? Stalling, mostly. Saying good-bye to Mom, yeah. I'd also like to say good-bye to Chris and Sarah. I'd like to take a long walk around the Point, stop in at all my favorite places. But I don't have time for any of that. And besides, I've got to believe I'm going to make it back.

I transfer the bone to my left hand, then dig into the sod with my right, worrying at it until I can peel a bit of it back.

Then I dig a little deeper with my fingers, push the bone into the rich dark dirt. I push it in as far as I can and cover it all over again. The last thing I do is pat the sod back into place.

I continue kneeling there for a long moment—expecting something—but nothing happens. There's no ghost voice in my head. I guess that only works in the magic lands.

"Good-bye, Mom," I say.

Then I stand up and return to where Johnny's waiting.

"Well," he says once we're back on the street and on our way to the B and B again, "looks like we've got something more in common than girlfriends that can turn into dogs."

I give him a surprised look. I knew his mother had run off and abandoned her family, but—

"I didn't know your mom died," I say.

"She didn't," he says. "I just meant that we both grew up without our mothers."

"I guess . . ."

I've never really thought about it before, what it must have been like for Johnny and his brother and sister, just coming home from school one day and finding their mother gone. There were times I felt like Mom had abandoned Dad and me, but I always knew deep down that it wasn't like she'd had any choice in the matter. She would never have voluntarily left us like Johnny's mother had her own family.

"It was the only smart thing she ever did," Johnny says, "because God knows marrying the old man sure wasn't."

"Do you miss her?" I find myself asking.

"She writes to me all the time," he says.

He looks at me, smiling at my surprise.

"Not at the house," he goes on. "The old man'd have a fit if he ever knew. Every so often I hitch out to my grandmother's place just outside of Tyson. That's where the letters come, and that's where I keep them. I keep my sketchbooks there, too, once they're filled."

"What about your brother and sister?" I ask. "Are they in touch with her, too?"

Johnny shakes his head. "Dave just shut the door on her when she left, and Sherry—hell, who knows what goes on in that head of hers besides sex, dope, and rock 'n' roll. No, as far's I know, it's only me."

"It must be hard," I say.

And then I realize he's got me doing it again. Getting me to empathize with him. But I can't take the words back now.

He shrugs. "Nothing good comes easy. That's what my grandmother says."

"Why don't you live with her?"

He's quiet for so long that I don't think he's going to answer.

"That's the pisser," he says. "I guess I've just got too much of the old man in me. I beat myself up about it, but at the same time, I like throwing my weight around. I like being the tough guy that the other kids have to be careful around." He shakes his head. "Ma doesn't know that side of me. She only knows my letters and the art I send her. Man, she'd hate me if she ever found out."

"So change."

He looks at me. "Fuck you, Schreiber."

We stop in the middle of the road, facing each other. I can see by the way he's standing, by the hunch of his shoulders, that he's ready to have a go at me again. But I don't want to fight him. I need to keep all my strength for when I have to stand up to Dingo. But I'm not going to cut him any slack, either.

"I don't know what Em saw in you," I say.

He stares at me for a long moment, then I can see the aggression just run off of him.

"Yeah," he says, his voice quiet. "Neither do I."

We fall silent again and continue on to the B and B, walking in the middle of the street, the town asleep around us, silent and dark. A few blocks from the house, I call Dad on my cell phone. He tells me that they're good to go. When I tell him where we are, he says that we should meet them on the beach. It makes sense, since at the moment, we're closer to the beach than we are to the B and B.

I pass the message on to Johnny as I clip my cell back onto my belt.

He nods but still has nothing to say as we turn down the next cross street that'll take us to Lighthouse Street and the long ridge that runs behind it, hiding the East Shore beach.

I thought I'd already dealt with my nervousness, but as soon as we step onto the beach, it all returns. I'm no hero. Johnny might be a tough guy, but, let's face it, we're just kids. What the hell are we doing here?

But I think of Lainey, and I know I have no choice.

Stephen and Dad are waiting for us by the water's edge a couple of hundred yards up the breach. I motion them over to where Johnny and I have stopped.

"This is about the right place, isn't it?" I ask Johnny.

He nods. "Yeah, I think this is where we landed. Or at least it's in spitting distance."

When Stephen and Dad join us, I turn to Stephen. It's impossible to know what's expected of us, what we're supposed to do here. He doesn't seem to be carrying any special gear or anything. He's just this surfer dude standing beside the old biker hippie that's my dad.

"You don't have do to anything," Stephen says when Johnny asks. "The leftover traces of your passage to get here are easy to find. Just relax, and remember what you need to do when you cross back over."

He looks at me when he says that last bit.

"Issue a challenge to Dingo," I say.

Stephen shakes his head. "Issue a *formal* challenge to Dingo. And invoke the bloodlines of your cousin kin. Black-winged crow and forest wolf."

"Crow and wolf. Got it."

"Though the bloodline might be coyote," Stephen says. "Better just to claim a connection to the canids in general."

I glance at Johnny, and he rolls his eyes at me. I know what he's thinking. It sounds ridiculous to me, too. Except we've both been in other worlds. We've both seen people turn into dingoes.

But, "Crow and canid," is all I say.

Stephen nods. "When you're ready, then."

Can you ever be ready for something like this? I wonder.

"Any time," Johnny says.

Dad takes a step toward me. "Miguel," he begins.

"I know," I tell him. "I'll be careful. Don't worry, Dad. We'll get this done and be back before you know it."

He looks as dubious as I feel, but all he does is give me a

quick hug, and we leave it at that. We both know this has to be done, and that circumstances being the way they are, only Johnny and I can do it.

Stephen doesn't wave his hands around, say some magic words, or really seem to do much of anything at all. He just looks at us, and the next thing I know, the beach is gone and we're dropping through the dark until we land back in the forest that is Dingo's giant tree. My stomach lurches, and I'm disoriented; there's a painful pressure in my chest. Then I realize that we're wrapped in those creepy branches again, the ones that seem to be as much flesh as they are bark and wood.

It's like no time at all has passed while we were gone. Dingo's face still looks out at us from the bark. The twins are still standing by the tree—they don't seem to have shifted their position at all. My heart lifts at the happy relief I see in Lainey's eyes. But Dingo. The face in the tree? Not so happy that we're back.

The branches tighten some more around my chest, and I know we're about to be flung away again, out of this world, back to the beach on the Point. I have this sudden fear that we'll get caught in a *Groundhog Day* loop, endlessly tossed back and forth between the worlds.

"Wait!" I call out. "We're—*I'm* here to issue a challenge—a formal challenge to you"—I have to think a moment to get his real name. "Warrigal. On the, um, honor of my cousin kin, the crows and canids."

Well, that was smoothly put.

The branches don't loosen, but they stop tightening. I have enough time to see the worried look on Lainey's face before Dingo's voice rings in my head and I turn to the face in the tree.

Boy, he says, his voice grim, *who have you been talking to?*

I swallow hard.

"That doesn't matter," I tell him. "Do you accept my challenge?"

The wooden mouth shapes a frown. *On my honor, you know I must. Can you say the same?*

"What do you mean?"

Trapped as I am, without a physical form, I must forfeit the challenge.

I nod. "We know that. So if you forfeit, we can all go, right?"

If you so decide. But on your honor, I request a proxy to take my place.

It's not like I wasn't expecting this. I know what Stephen says we should do. I know what the smart thing to do is.

I look at the twins. Em's shaking her head as she realizes that I'm actually considering it. Lainey has an expression that I can't read, but she's probably thinking what I am: Go with the plan, we all get to go home, end of story, complete with happy ending.

But going the easy route doesn't feel right.

"Don't be a total chump," Johnny says. "He's just psyching you."

Maybe he is, maybe he isn't. But I've already made up my mind.

I find myself wishing that there'd been time to appreciate all the amazing things that have happened to me. Lainey's love and her shape-shifting abilities. All these other worlds that have to have more to them than weird trees. Trees full of bones. Trees that can come to life. Trees with a man's head in their trunk that moves and speaks with a voice in your head.

But it's been a headlong rush of one action into another, with no time to stop and really experience the wonder and magic of it all. That's just the way it goes sometimes.

"This proxy," I say. "He'll be human and my age, right? No magic, no superpowers. Just a kid like me."

I see something I didn't expect in Dingo's eyes. Respect.

Of course, he says.

"And it doesn't have to be a, you know, fight to the death or anything, right? Just whoever cries 'uncle' first."

I'm not sure where that expression ever came from, but Dingo seems to be familiar with it.

If that is your wish, he says.

"Jesus," Johnny says. "What the hell are you doing?"

"I'm doing what's right," I say, without looking at him.

"Yeah, like he ever would."

"It doesn't matter," I say. "It's what I need to do."

I look at the twins. Em seems resigned to my stupidity, but she gives me a thumbs-up when she catches my gaze on her. Lainey looks proud, if a little nervous. I don't blame her. I'm nervous, too.

I turn back to Dingo.

"Okay," I tell him. "Bring on your pinch hitter."

Dingo's gaze moves from me to Johnny.

I asked for your help in your dreams, he says to Johnny. *Now I ask you again: Will you help me?*

Johnny laughs. "What—you want me to beat him up for you?"

I want you to be my proxy in this challenge, yes.

Johnny looks at me, and in his eyes I catch a glimpse of the mean-spirited bully I know so well from school and the streets of the Point.

"And if I do," he asks Dingo, "it's the same deal? I get whatever I want from you?"

You have my word.

"Which everybody seems to think is golden, so I guess I can take it to the bank."

"Johnny!" Em cries. "Don't do this."

He turns to her. "Why not? I don't know where any of this crap is taking us. Do you care for me? Were you just using me? I mean, nothing's clear anymore. But hitting somebody—that I understand."

"I did care for you . . ."

"Yeah, that's why we're here in this place."

I can't believe he's being so pigheadedly stupid. So . . . so Johnny Ward. How can he not see that she genuinely cared for him? Maybe the twins weren't entirely forthcoming about the situation when we first hooked up with them, but when do you start to tell your potential boyfriend that you can change into a dingo, and, oh yeah, there are supernatural forces trying to take you down? If it was me, it sure wouldn't be the first thing I'd tell anybody.

But apparently Johnny doesn't care about any of that. He's thinking only of himself.

He turns his back on the twins to face me. "So, you and me, Schreiber. Think you can take me?"

We both know I can't. He already proved that on the beach earlier. So I don't bother to reply. There's no point in arguing the right or wrong of this. Johnny's got his schoolyard face on, and the only thing he knows right now is that might makes right.

I clench my fists. I'm so not one of the heroes in my

dad's comic books. I wish I was. I wish I was strong and indestructible. That I could put on some magic ring—or yell "Shazam!"—and just take down the villain without even getting out of breath. But that's not going to happen here.

Johnny walks toward me and puts out his hand.

"May the best man win and all that crap, right?" he says.

I go to shake his hand, and he sucker punches me with his left.

It's so fast, I never see it coming. The blow catches me on the side of my mouth and staggers me. I literally see stars and taste my own blood. But there's no time to deal with the pain because Johnny's already swinging again. I duck into the blow so it can't connect, and then we're grappling.

He's stronger than me, but I've got this on my side: complete and utter panic that if I don't win this, Lainey and Em are lost. The trouble is, hanging on to him doesn't do anything except postpone the inevitable.

"Jesus, you're such a wuss," Johnny says before he pushes me away.

He gets in another shot to my head, and I see those stars again. He doesn't follow through quickly enough, and I charge him once more, this time with my head down. The move takes him by surprise, and I manage to get in a good head butt. Then before he can get away, I bring my fist up, hard and fast, and drive it into his crotch.

I know that had to hurt. It should have been enough for me at least to catch my breath and clear my head. But pain doesn't seem to immobilize a Ward the way it does anyone else. Instead, it drives him into a rage.

He comes at me, raining blows. I try to block them, but too many get through. I take so many shots to the head that I lose all sense of direction and purpose. I stumble back, disoriented and stupid with the pain. And then I'm lying on the ground. I don't even know how I got there, or when I fell.

I try to get up, but all that gets me is a kick in the side. Once, twice.

I don't think I've ever hurt so much before.

There's sweat in my eyes, which are already half closed and swollen. I can't really see where Johnny is, but I try to get up again anyway.

A foot comes down on my chest, pinning me to the ground. I try to wriggle out from under it, and the foot moves to my throat. I gag as it presses down on me.

"I'm impressed," Johnny says. "But really. This is where it ends."

"Stop hurting him!" I hear Lainey cry.

"Well, now," Johnny says, "that's up to your boyfriend. What do you say, Schreiber? You had enough yet?"

I can't talk with his foot on my throat. I make a grab for it, and the sudden increase of pressure makes me gag again.

"Man, now's the time to—how did you put it?—cry 'uncle.'" The pressure eases on my throat, and I gulp some air. "You ready to call it a day?"

I shake my head. I'm hopelessly outclassed and have no strength, but I refuse to give up.

Johnny's face comes up close to mine as he bends down. I stare up at him through my half-shut eyes.

"You should," Johnny says.

I don't see the fist coming, but I feel it as it rocks my head to one side.

"I can keep this up all day," he says.

And hits me again.

"That's enough!" Em cries. "You win, okay? So just leave him alone."

Johnny stays where he is for a long moment, fist cocked. I try to signal that I'm beaten. Then he shrugs and stands up.

Lainey runs over and kneels down, cradling my head on her lap. She brushes the hair from my brow with feather-light fingers.

"My poor brave boy," she whispers.

"No. I . . . I'm a loser . . ."

"Don't you *ever* say that."

"Yeah," Em puts in. I never heard her approach. "It's not

your fault that the psycho boy hurt you. Hurting people's the only thing he's good at doing."

The two of them help me sit up. The pain is everywhere, but mostly inside, in my heart. It doesn't matter what the twins say. I let them down.

Johnny has his back to us. Arms folded across his chest, he faces Dingo.

"So now what?" he asks.

You claim your prize, Dingo tells him.

"Anything I want, right? How's that work anyway? I mean, if you're, like, such a powerful magic genie man, why are you stuck in that tree?"

It's complicated.

"Yeah, I'll bet it is. So . . . whatever I want. What if I said I want us all to go free and you never to bug us again."

The twins and I look at him with surprise. Dingo hesitates for a long moment.

If that's your wish, he finally says.

Now it's Johnny's turn to fall silent.

Well? Dingo asks.

"First things first," Johnny says. "You were telling me how you ended up in that tree."

I don't believe I was.

"Yeah, but you're going to do it all the same."

Don't push your luck, boy.

"First off," Johnny says, "don't you ever call me 'boy' again. And secondly, tell me what I want to know, or my wish is going to be that you rot in some burning hell for all eternity."

Oh, the face in the tree is pissed off, no question.

You're playing a dangerous game, Dingo tells Johnny.

Johnny shrugs. "Still not hearing what I want to hear."

This goes back a long time ago, Dingo says, *back to the days of the long ago when the only people were animals, and we were all still settling on our shapes. Sun Woman had three sons, and it was said that they knew words that could give you the shape you wanted. All you had to do was catch them in a good mood and ask.*

"I read that dingoes first came to Australia with Asian seafarers," Johnny says, "which was only four thousand years ago. That's not exactly at the beginning of time. Hell, the Aborigines had already been there for over forty thousand years."

I realize that after his Australian dreams, Johnny did a bunch of research, too—just as I did.

Who's telling this story? Dingo asks.

Johnny shrugs. "I'm just saying. The fossil records don't show that there were any of you in Australia until four thousand years ago."

By human accounting.

"Hey, a fact's a fact. If you'd been there, there'd be fossil records."

Unless we didn't start dying *until four thousand years ago.*

"How's that possible?"

Maybe if you listened more and talked less, you'd learn something.

Johnny gives another shrug. "So, go on. I'm all ears."

Back then, Kanga—the first kangaroo—wasn't a whole lot different from anybody else, and he didn't like that. He had four short legs and a skinny little tail, but he wanted to be special. He kept bugging Sun Woman's three sons to make him different. He wanted to be wonderfully popular and run after. You know, anybody saw him, they'd just want to be like him, or just to be with him. He wanted everybody chasing after him, looking to be his friend,

The boys got so sick of his pestering, the oldest of the three came to me and asked me if I could help.

"All you need to do is chase him for one day," he tells me. "Don't let him rest, don't let him stop, and we'll see he gets to be something between what he wants so bad and what he deserves."

Well, we're talking Sun Woman's boys here—I'm going to say no? I chased that old roo from one side of the country to another. We got to a river and he hopped across on his hind legs, and then I guess he took a liking to that way of movement, because he tucked in his front legs, stuck out his tail for balance, and kept on hopping along on his hind legs. I didn't let him stop or rest. So as the day went by, those hind legs of his grew longer and stronger, his tail got big and fat, and his front legs all but disappeared, they got so small.

Finally, the day ended, and we could rest. Kanga bends down at a pool of water for a drink and oh, is he pissed when he has a look at his new self. He looks like a fool, his little upper body sitting there on top of these big old legs and tail.

"Why are you complaining?" the oldest of Sun Woman's boys asks when Kanga comes to him. "You wanted to be different—well, I gave you that."

"Not like this," Kanga says.

Sun Woman's boy shrugs and turns away. "Not my problem," he calls over his shoulder.

Well naturally, Kanga blames me, because all the roo cousins from then on are born looking like him. Big ones and little ones. Paddymelons and wallabies and big old red roos.

Now he's big and strong, but I'm fast and smart, and there's no way he can ever catch me. So he does something worse. He goes deep into the bush and finds the place where death is buried and digs it up with those big hind legs of his. Digs it up and brings it back to where we all live.

So now dingoes can die, but so can roos, and we've been enemies ever since.

"That's it?" Johnny says when Dingo falls silent. "Are you serious? Could you be more *Aesop's Fables*? I didn't ask for you to tell me 'How the Kangaroo Got Its Great Big Frickin' Legs' or any of that other crap."

I believe it was Kipling who appropriated this particular story of mine, not Aesop.

"What-friggin'-ever. I just want to know how you ended up in this tree."

For a long moment I don't think Dingo is going to answer. Then he finally says, *One day I wasn't fast or smart enough. Kanga caught me on my own and used a piece of some old root magic he'd been hoarding away in that pouch of his. He sent me here, into this dreaming time, and bound me into this tree.* He pauses a moment, then adds. *The old fig wasn't so big then, but I've been here for a very long time.*

There you have my story—the whole and the true of it.

"And the only way you can get free is how, exactly?"

Oh, Kanga was clever with that as well. He knew the blood-lines were getting thin because dingo cousins were mating with too many feral dogs. So he bound into the magic the condition that I could be freed only by the blood of my most pure-blooded descendant.

"Which at the present time is the twins."

Yes.

His wooden gaze shifts to where I'm sitting with Lainey and Em on either side of me, before it goes back to Johnny.

I'm not happy about it, Dingo says, *but I've been trapped in this tree for a long, long time.*

Johnny nods. "I get that." Now he looks over to us. "You girls believe this crappy story?" he asks.

Em's so shocked at the question she forgets how angry she is with him.

"Of course," she says. "Dingo can't lie."

Johnny smiles. "Naïve much?"

"You don't understand," Lainey tells. "Cousins don't lie."

"Never?"

"Not if they give their word like Dingo did."

Let's finish our business, Dingo says, breaking in. *Tell me what you want from me.*

"That's a tough call. I can have just, literally, anything, right?"

Anything. Wealth, women, a long and bountiful life.

"And how's that work?"

I don't understand.

"You're magic enough to grant me whatever wish I want, but you can't step out of that tree on your own."

I'm an old dingo, the oldest of my clan. I can do many

things, work many magics. But because of Kanga's spell, I can't work them for myself.

Johnny nods. "Okay. I get that. So what I want is you free from this tree so that all this crap of you chasing the girls ends here."

But . . .

"Hey, it's fulfilling the requirement. The twins carry your blood, and because of them, I'm here. So you're being freed by their blood. Did Kanga say anything about it having to be spilled?"

No.

"Then step out of that friggin' tree already so that we can all go home."

Lainey's been holding my hand. Her fingers tighten on mine. Em takes my other hand, and the two girls look at each other across me. I don't think any of us quite believe Johnny's change of heart. Unless, I think, it wasn't a change of heart. Unless he'd had this planned all along.

"What are you waiting for?" Johnny asks.

I . . . Dingo's voice seems unsure, then grows more firm: *Nothing.*

The girls and I get to our feet as the wooden face pushes farther out of the tree. I smell something funny in the air, like an electric circuit that's gotten too hot and is about to burn out. The face starts to shift into flesh. The whole head's out now, one hand, the forearm. Another hand. The front of his chest.

Then suddenly he's a man, falling out of the tree, flesh and blood, lean and wiry, with a head of red-gold hair. He would have hit the ground, but Johnny's there to catch him.

"Le-legs . . . don't . . . seem . . . to . . . work . . ." Dingo says in a voice that's also raspy from disuse.

Johnny settles him on the ground, and Dingo leans back against the giant fig that had been his prison.

"You'll get your strength back," Johnny says.

Dingo looks up at him with eyes as deep and dark brown as Lainey's and Em's. "Thank you," he tells Johnny.

"Whatever. Are we good now? No more debts, no more threats?"

"Of course."

"Okay. So, here's a plan. Why don't you just give me back my old man's rifle and send us home."

"I will. Just let me catch my breath and gather a little strength first."

It's such a relief not to have his voice ringing in my head.

Johnny looks at us. I don't see an ounce of remorse in him for having just beat the crap out of me. But then I guess Johnny Ward's never apologized for anything in his whole life. Why would he start now?

"You guys good with that?" he asks.

Em turns away so that she doesn't have to look at him. She and Lainey are both standing close to me, as though I can protect them, but as Johnny's already proven, there's fat chance of that.

Since neither of them responds to him, I nod.

"Yeah, sure," I say.

"What will you do now, Warrigal?" Lainey asks Dingo.

He gives her a thin smile. "Do you mean, will I now go take my revenge on Kanga and let the cycle begin all over again?" He shakes his head. "I plan to do nothing. I plan to walk and run and breathe and eat and drink and do all the things denied to me in my tree prison."

"Yeah, well that's all really exciting," Johnny says. "I'm going to go look for my old man's rifle. You just give a shout when you're ready to send us back home."

We watch him disappear through the thicket of the fig tree's boughs.

"Are you going to be okay?" Lainey asks me. "Does anything feel broken?"

"Because you don't look so good," Em adds.

I'd be surprised if I did. Both eyes are swelling shut, and every part of me seems to hurt.

"I might have a cracked rib," I say. "It hurts if I take too deep a breath."

It's hard to talk. My mouth and cheeks are swollen, my jaw aches, and I think I've got a couple of loose teeth. Getting beat up this badly sure isn't anything like the way they show it in the movies.

We walk over to where Dingo is sitting, the twins supporting me on either side. I don't know if moving is such a good idea. I feel all rubbery after a few steps, and the world keeps doing these slow spins. Without help, I'm sure I would have gone sprawling after two steps. The girls lower me onto the grass when we get to the main trunk of the fig, then sit beside me.

Dingo seems to have about as much energy as I do. He looks as though the only thing keeping him sitting upright is the trunk of the tree against his back. But his dark gaze is still full of strength.

"Your cousin blood might be thin," he tells me, "but you did your tribes proud today."

I have trouble focusing on his features, but getting off my feet has at least cleared my head a little. If I keep my breathing shallow, my chest almost doesn't hurt. I just want to lie down and sleep for a week, but I force myself to speak.

"I'm sure," I say. "I'm sure they'd be real impressed with how I got the crap kicked out of me."

Dingo shakes his head. "You could have made me

forfeit your challenge, but instead you did the honorable thing. That's not something any cousin takes lightly."

"I guess."

"Your companion surprised me, too."

"Yeah, Johnny's a real piece of work, all right. He's probably just been waiting to give me a good pounding."

"I didn't mean that," Dingo says. "I meant that instead of taking something for himself, he gave me my freedom."

Considering the way I feel at the moment, I'm not particularly impressed with Johnny's big moment of selflessness.

"I don't understand how that worked," Em says. "If you could just step out of the tree when Johnny said that's what he wanted for his wish, why couldn't you do it anytime?"

He shrugs. "It's as I told you earlier. My own magic doesn't work for me. And in all those years inside this old fig, it never occurred to me that I could lend my magic to another to free me."

"No, you just wanted to kill us," Lainey says.

"That's not true."

"You were after our blood. It's kind of hard to get it without killing us first."

Dingo gives us another shrug. "To be honest, I'm not sure how it would have worked. I simply knew that I needed pure-blooded descendants, and they had to help me willingly." He hesitates a moment, then adds, "I thought you would be taking my place in the tree."

"And you thought we'd do that willingly?" Em says.

Lainey shakes her head. "Of course, he didn't. He was going to trick us into doing it."

"Like blackmailing you by kidnapping your stepdad," I say.

From the shock on their faces, I realize that the twins didn't know about that, so I fill them in on what happened back at the B and B.

"I didn't ask Tallyman to do that," Dingo says.

If he can't lie, I guess we have to believe that.

"So why would he?" Lainey asks.

Em nods. "Yeah, what would the creep get out of it?"

"He was currying favor," Dingo tells them. "By helping me, he would put me in his debt. It's simple as that."

"And you were okay with that?" I ask. "You were okay with him fathering a kid to take your place in the tree?"

"I was in that tree for a very long time."

"Oh, and that makes it right?"

A dark look comes into his eye that reminds me of the horrible nightmare he gave me a couple of days ago. The woman in my bed who turned into a long-dead corpse, dropping maggots onto my face.

"Don't push me too hard, boy," he says.

I don't like being called "boy" anymore than Johnny does, but I decide not to press it just now. I turn my face away.

"I will see that Tallyman leaves you alone now," Dingo says.

"Good," Em says.

We fall silent then until we hear footsteps in the brush and look up to see Johnny return, his father's rifle in hand. He gives us all a once-over. I suppose we should be thankful that he saved the day. Dingo's free. The threat to the twins is gone. But did he have to do it the way that he did?

My aches and bruises won't let me feel as grateful as I know I should. I mean, I *wanted* the twins to be safe, but right now I hurt too much, and I'm not particularly happy to see him again. Lainey seems to have the same conflict running through her mind, because as soon as he comes into sight, she takes my hand and gently strokes the back of it with her fingers. I smile at her as best as I can with my swollen lips, then turn to look at Em. She doesn't seem any happier to see Johnny than we are.

"Well, aren't we a happy gang," he says.

"You didn't have to beat Miguel up," Em tells him.

"No, I pretty much did, seeing as how he was too stupid to stick with the plan."

"You know why he couldn't," Lainey says.

Johnny shrugs. "He didn't have to let it go as far as it did. He could have stopped it anytime. After all, I was doing it for you guys."

"How was he supposed to know that?"

"He could have trusted me to do the right thing." He smiles without any humor. "You know, the way I was supposed to trust you."

No one says anything in response, but we're all thinking the same thing: Why were we supposed to trust him, when everything he said and did gave us a completely different message?

"Or you could have stopped it," Lainey says, "except you needed to get a few extra shots in, didn't you? Maybe to get back at his father for kicking you out of his store."

Johnny shrugs. "Whatever. Can we go now?"

"Is that true?" Em asks. "Is that really why—"

Johnny cuts her off. "So are you ready to send us back, Dingo?"

"I think so."

Dingo gets to his feet slowly, using the tree trunk at his back to help him stand. The twins help me to my feet.

"Thank you for your help," Dingo says, "and I'm sorry for all the trouble I've brought into your life."

Trouble? I think. Yeah, maybe. But if he hadn't been

chasing the twins, I wouldn't have Lainey in my life, either. A bunch of weirdness and getting beat up's a fair trade for that.

And then the blackness comes sweeping in, and we're back on the beach again, just the four of us, the first hint of dawn pinking the sky above the lake.

Dad freaks, of course, when he sees the shape I'm in. I hurt everywhere. My eyes are swollen so much that I can't see out of them at all, and I have to depend on Lainey to guide me across the stones to where Dad and Stephen are standing.

"It . . . it's not as bad as it looks," I try to tell Dad, but he doesn't buy it for a moment.

He takes Lainey's place and leads me away, back to our house, leaving everybody else behind on the beach. When we get home, he starts up the truck and we go directly to the hospital. The last time I was there was when Chris broke his arm falling out of a tree. I didn't like it then, and I like it less now, with all the attention on me.

They give me a shot for the pain and keep me overnight, even though the X-rays come back and show that nothing's broken. I spend the night in a room, but I don't sleep well. I'm sharing my room with a guy whose coughing keeps waking me up, and the nurse comes in once an hour to make sure I don't have a concussion. But they release me in the morning, scrubbed with disinfectants and ready to heal.

Lainey's with Dad when he comes to pick me up, and they bring me back to the house.

"You look terrible," Lainey says.

I can actually see a little bit through the swelling, so I know what she means. When I looked in the mirror this morning, I almost couldn't recognize myself. The glass cast back a reflection of something from a horror film.

"Well, you look great," I tell her.

Dad laughs. "Now I'm relieved. If you're feeling good enough to compliment your girlfriend, then I know you're going to be okay."

I'm off school for a week, but I have the constant companionship of Nurse Lainey during my waking hours. Sometimes Em comes by as well. She's still quiet and a little distant, but I know now it's got nothing to do with me. She's just trying to figure out the walking contradiction that is Johnny Ward, and her own conflicted feelings toward him.

Welcome to the club, I want to tell her. I don't, because I know it won't help. The weirdest thing is, even after the beating Johnny gave me, I look at her sad face and want to figure out some way to get the two of them together again.

I think I know why Johnny became Dingo's proxy so enthusiastically. It wasn't me he was hitting. It was the whole world that's forever conspiring against him.

I was his father. I was everybody who expected him to be the bully, those expectations keeping him from being the artist he thinks he really is, if he could only have the chance. I was the yellow streak of cowardice that stopped him from rising above the self he showed the world.

I think that when Johnny was beating me up, I was just standing in for the guy he really wanted to be hitting: himself.

That didn't make what he did right. But when you understand why someone's done a terrible thing, it can't help but change the way you feel.

Chris and Sarah are completely enamored of Lainey and Em, and why wouldn't they be? The twins are cute and smart and funny and have those adorable accents, though they continue to insist that they speak perfectly normally, thank you very much. We're the ones who have the accents.

It's hard for me, keeping secrets from my best friends, but all I've told them is that Johnny and I were double-dating the twins on the beach; that things were going well until Johnny and I got into a fight. What else could I have said? How do you even start explaining other worlds and were-dingoes?

But it puts a little distance between us, and that hurts. And it doesn't go unnoticed.

"It's like you guys are in on some secret that nobody else gets," Chris says to me one day before Lainey comes over.

"We don't mean to be," I tell him.

"Dude, it's cool. You're in love, L-U-V. You've just got to tell me that you don't have some kind of kinky threesome deal going on, or I am going to be so frigging jealous."

I laugh. "I thought you were in love with Sarah."

"I totally am. But how much cooler would it be if there were two of her?"

"It's so not like that," I tell him. "Lainey and Em are completely different people."

"Who look *exactly* the same, dude."

I shake my head. "I don't know why I bother." Then I cock my head and ask, "Does Sarah know about this little fantasy of yours?"

"Come on, dude. Don't start with the blackmail. I'd hate to have to hit a guy who's already black and blue from head to toe."

Sarah's got a whole other concern with the twins, but I make her promise to back off before she can go all matchmaker on Em.

"Give her time to get over Johnny," I say.

"Johnny's not something you get over," Sarah says. "He's a disease that you have to put right out of your memory, and the best way to do that is to fall in love with someone else."

"You make it sound so easy. Falling in love, I mean."

"Well, everybody knows it's not. But you don't even have the chance of it happening if all you do is spend your time at home, walking alone on the beach, or visiting the friend that your boyfriend beat up."

"Just promise me you'll wait a while before you try to hook her up with every perfect guy you know."

Sarah smiles. "I only know two of them," she says, "and they're already taken."

I don't know who blushes more—Chris or me. Because we can see from the warmth in her eyes that she totally means it.

"But I promise," she says.

By the time I go back to school, the swellings have mostly gone and my purples, blacks, and blues are pale yellows and greens. I'm still sore, but it's not as bad as it was for the first few days.

I already know the word went around that it was Johnny who'd done this to me—you don't keep many secrets in a town as small as the Point. As soon as I get back, I can feel everybody waiting for the two of us to meet somewhere in the halls and have another go at each other.

If circumstances had been different, it would probably work that way. That's another thing about small towns—you tend to fall into people's expectations of what you're going to do. But Johnny keeps out of my way, and revenge isn't high on my list of priorities. Sure, I'm still sore, and Johnny totally humiliated me in front of Lainey. But at the end of the day, I just feel sorry for him.

I'm with Lainey.

He isn't with Em anymore because he'd done worse than getting humiliated in front of his girlfriend.

I don't think Johnny's avoiding a confrontation with me so much as he's avoiding the pity he knows he'll see in my eyes.

We each get fifteen minutes of fame, they say. Or at least of public interest. I didn't think I'd get even that once the twins enrolled at Harnett High. I figured that seeing a bruised and battered Miguel Schreiber walking the halls of the school would be no match for the interest they'd generate.

I'm half right. Everybody wants to hang with them or,

at the very least, is checking them out, but since they've attached themselves to Chris, Sarah, and me, suddenly we're on everybody's radar as well.

It's kind of fun being popular, if only by association. The twins take it in stride, charming everyone with their good nature and accents. But I see that it's wearing on Em. Everything's a reminder to her that she's on her own: the two couples that Chris and Sarah and Lainey and I make; all the guys hitting on her.

But she's not interested in meeting guys. Her heart's still aching because of Johnny. Her anger's long gone, and all's that left is a sadness that won't go away.

I finally decide that, for Em's sake, I need to talk to him, but I don't get the chance until a day in late October. Dad and I are at the store, pricing a box of Vertigo trade paperbacks that he got at an estate sale, when I see Johnny go by. He's heading south on Main Street, which'll take him to the town square.

"I need to run an errand," I tell Dad.

He nods, only half paying attention to what I'm saying. There's a complete run of *Sandman* trades in the box, and he's been flipping through them to look at the art. He doesn't need to read them for the stories since he's already read them a half-dozen times before, in these and various other editions.

He glances up at me, still distracted.

"You'll be home for supper?" he asks.

"Sure."

If Johnny doesn't kill me.

I slip out of the store and follow Johnny, keeping well back so he won't spot me. When he gets to the town square, he cuts across the parking lot to the public beach. I loiter behind some cars until he gets to the end of the sand. As soon as he disappears among the rocks, I jog across the beach. I don't see him when I reach the rocks myself. He blends in with the rocks in his faded jeans and gray jacket, and it takes me a few moments to spot him, hunched in a hollow of granite and limestone, his sketchbook open on his lap.

I pick my way over the rocks. I know he hears me coming, but he doesn't lift his head. On the open page of his sketchbook is a half-done drawing of Em—obviously drawn from memory, since he's got her wearing the jean skirt with the striped blue-and-white stockings that she had on at school today. I'm no art expert, but the drawing looks really good.

"Hey," I say.

He finally acknowledges my presence with a cold look.

"The fuck do you want?" he says.

"Just to talk."

"Yeah, like I'm going to be scared if we go round two."

"Why do you have to be like this?" I ask.

"You mean be who I am?"

"You know what I mean."

"Oh," he says, "you want me to be more like the sensitive artist I've got hidden away behind this mask of toughness and anger."

"When you put it like that . . ."

He nods. "Exactly. It sounds like a load of crap. I'm just who I am, Schreiber. I could cry about never catching a break, but so what? This is my world, and I'm stuck in it. Some things never change. Things might seem like they're going my way for a while, but it never sticks."

"It doesn't have to be that black and white."

"Except it is. And it's always going to go to crap in the end. That business with Dingo in the tree is the perfect example. I save the day, but you get the girl. Hell, you might have both of them, for all I know."

"Nobody's saying you didn't save the day," I tell him. "It's just how you did it."

"Like I should have thrown the fight so that you could be the hero?"

"I don't mean that. It's just—"

201

"And would you have set Dingo free?"

"It's not something I ever thought—"

"Because from where I'm standing, what I did worked out a whole lot better than your plan would've."

I touch where the bruises were on my face. "It's just—"

"Were you going to give in? Hell, you never did. Em had to call it quits for you."

"If you'd just communicated what you were planning—"

"I was improvising, man. And even if I'd had a plan, I wouldn't have shared it with you, because then it wouldn't have been seemed real, and it's pretty obvious that Dingo has a nose for the truth."

"So why don't you tell Em all of this?"

"She doesn't want jack from me."

"Have you even *tried* to talk to her?"

"Come on. You saw the look on her face the same as I did."

"Maybe. But I'm also seeing the look on her face these past few weeks, totally bumming because she just doesn't get who you are."

"Yeah, well, I don't get her, either. Or maybe I get her all too well."

"Just talk to her."

"Why do you care?"

"About you? Not so much. But I care about her. She doesn't deserve this."

"No," he says. "We can't have things not go her way for a change."

"What the hell's that supposed to mean?

"Come on, are you that naïve? Do those girls look like they ever didn't get what they wanted just by batting their eyes and making a few promises?"

I shake my head. "You're throwing away the chance for something really good."

"Oh, so if I talk to her, everything's going to work out just fine?"

"I can't promise that."

"Of course you can't. So why don't you just take a hike, Schreiber? Or maybe you're ready for another go at me?"

I ignore that.

"But if you don't talk to her," I say, "you'll never know, will you? Maybe you guys will get together again, and maybe you won't. But what I do know is that she's unhappy, you're unhappy, and if you don't try, you're both going to stay that way for sure."

"Easy for you to say. You've never—"

"Lived my life like I'm a loser? Yeah. You're right. I never have."

He lays the sketchbook down and gets to his feet. "You want to fight?" he asks.

I keep my hands by my sides. "No," I tell him, "but you go ahead and hit me a few more times if it's going to make you feel better."

For a moment I think he's going to do just that, but then he shakes his head.

"I don't get you, Schreiber," he says. "I know you're not a coward."

"You mean because I won't fight you?"

He nods.

"Maybe I only fight for things I believe in, instead of just for the fun of it."

"You think I don't have things I believe in?"

"I don't know. Isn't Em worth fighting for?"

"What the hell's that supposed to mean?"

He looks genuinely confused.

"Just go talk to her," I say.

Then I walk away.

True to his word, Dingo must have called off Tallyman, because the twins' biological father certainly leaves them alone. Me? Not so much. I guess Tallyman still has his own ideas about debts owed and payback. Johnny doesn't seem to be on his radar—maybe because he hadn't been there when Tallyman was being duct-taped to a chair—but apparently I'm fair game.

The first time I see him stalking me, I'm walking home alone from the store, heading up MacHatton Street to drop in on Lainey. Tallyman's the last thing on my mind until I see him loping down the street toward me. At first I think it's Lainey or Em, playing a trick on me, but the growls are too real, and the look in the dingo's eyes is a serious anger, so I know who it is.

I have a moment of real panic. Do I run? Too late for that. Do I fight? To what end?

But then this pack of crows comes dropping out of the sky. There must be a couple of dozen of them, cawing and pecking at the dingo until they've driven it off. Then they wheel off with almost military precision, dipping their wings at me in a salute before they sail off into the sky once more and are gone.

I'd like to say I take it all in stride, but instead I just stand there with my mouth open and a look of stupidity splashed all over my face. I don't know which surprised me more: Tallyman's attack, or the crows' rescue. When I tell Lainey about it, she smiles and pokes me in the chest with a stiff finger.

"It's your cousin blood," she says.

I give her a blank look.

That gets me another finger poke.

"You know," she says. "Dingo must have sent word to the corbae, and now they're looking out for you."

"Yeah, right."

"Do you have a better explanation?"

"Not really. But . . . come on. Why would they care about me?"

"Because you're brave and smart, and you did them proud?"

"I love having my own personal cheerleader," I tell her, "but I'm not sure you're right."

Except after that I start noticing the birds—these corbae cousins whose blood I'm supposed to share. I can't go anywhere without spying at least one of them somewhere in my line of sight. Crows and ravens, blue jays, rooks and jackdaws. They'll be sitting in a tree, or high on a phone wire, or maybe up on the corner of some building. Watching me. Watching *out* for me, I suppose, but it still feels like I'm stuck in that old Hitchcock flick, and it gives me the creeps.

Until the next time Tallyman makes a try for me.

This time I'm alone on the beach—just kicking around. I hadn't lied to Lainey way back when. I actually do like coming out along the East Shore on my own, feeling the wind on my face and skipping stones out over the lake.

So there I am, a nice flat stone in my hand, when I see

the dingo running in my direction. My gaze goes up, and, sure enough, there are crows circling up there. They come swooping down on the dingo, raucous caws filling the air. I don't know where they all come from, but in moments there are dozens of the black birds attacking the dingo.

Oh, he doesn't like it. I watch Tallyman dodge back and forth, jaws snapping at the birds, but he doesn't even come close to getting one of them. Drops of blood splatter on his fur from where the birds are pecking at him, until he finally turns tail and beats a quick retreat back down the shore. Half the birds follow him, jeering and cawing. Those that remain do their wing salute for me. This time I raise a hand and call out my thanks before they sail off, riding the wind like a gang of airborne sailboarders, tacking back and forth along the air currents.

After that I always give them a wave. Sometimes I even say hello, which, when I'm with Chris or Sarah, gets me a "Dude!" or a curious look. But those birds, they always bob their heads or ruffle their wing feathers in my direction.

Now the funny thing is, even after all I've been through—and with the corbae so obviously looking out for me—I'm still not exactly walking around thinking about magic all the time. Sure, I know now that there's more to the world than I can usually see, but normal life goes on. It's not like Lainey or Em are constantly shifting into their dingo shapes in front of me. Tallyman's always a dingo when he tries to ambush me. When I open a door, I find just what I expect to find on the other side, not some mystical otherworld with haunted baobab trees or an Australian rain forest with a talking turkey.

So the supernatural is pretty much the last thing on my mind until Lainey says she wants to meet my mother.

"That's not funny," I say, but then I give her a searching look and add, "Are you saying you could talk to her?"

"The same as you can," she replies, "though who knows if she'll be listening. Most spirits move on pretty quickly from this world. But it seems like introducing myself to her would be the polite thing to do, even if she's not there to hear me."

That doesn't make a whole lot of sense, but then the twins are forever coming out with things that don't seem particularly logical on the surface. And I like the fact that Lainey wants to come to my mother's grave.

So the next day after school I take her to the small graveyard behind Our Lady of Sorrows Church. Before coming to school, Lainey picked some purple asters from her garden and kept them in a jar of water in her locker during the day. They're a little worse for the wear by now, but I know Mom would still like them.

"It's the small kindnesses that make the biggest difference," she always liked to say.

It's another gray day in the Point, but as Lainey and I walk hand in hand between the gravestones, my heart is lighter than any other time I've been here. I'm still sad Mom is gone—I mean, you never get over that, do you?—but I'm not here by myself. And Lainey knows just how I'm feeling, because she lost her own mother.

When we get to Mom's grave, we sit on the grass in front of the headstone. Lainey runs her finger across the inscription.

"Dalila Perez-Schreiber," she reads. She looks at me and adds, "It's a beautiful name."

I never really thought about it. She was always just "Mom" to me. But I nod in agreement.

Lainey cocks her head as though she hears something she can't quite identify.

"There are a lot of spirits around here," she says after a moment. "I can hear them murmuring all around us."

"Is . . . do you hear my mother?"

"I can't tell. There are too many voices to pick out just one."

Too many voices, I think. Then I remember the finger bone that I brought back from the baobab tree. I tell Lainey how I buried it here, because this was the most sacred ground I could think of.

She smiles. "That's why they seem so familiar. Now shush a moment."

Sitting on her haunches, she lays her flowers on the grass in front of the headstone.

"Hello, Ms. Perez-Schreiber," she says. "You don't know me, but I'm starting to get to know a little about you through Miguel. My name's Lainey Howe, and I'm Miguel's girl-friend." She turns to me and smiles before going on, "Actually, we're betrothed, but we won't be getting married for a long time. We need to finish school and stuff first. But I just wanted to introduce myself to you, and to make you this promise: I'm going to do whatever I can to take care of Miguel and make him happy, just as I know he'll do the same for me.

"I . . . I wish I could have met you. Maybe you could look up my mother. I'm sure she'll vouch for me. I . . . "

When her voice trails off, I reach over and take her hand.

"You're very cool," I tell her. "A little weird, but very cool."

"Why?" she asks, squeezing my fingers. "Because I talk to ghosts?"

"And can turn into a dingo. And can open a door into another world."

"Regrets?"

I shake my head. "I wouldn't want you any other way. I just hope that my mom heard you, and that she and your mom can meet."

I will take your message to her, a familiar voice says in my head. *You are a man of your word. This is a blessed place for fellas like us.*

Lainey looks around to see who's speaking, but I don't because I know. I lay my free hand on the grass. Somewhere, under grass blades and roots and dirt, a little bone lies buried, and spirits are free.

"Thanks," I say.

Lainey lays her free hand on top of mine.

"You're a bit weird, too," she says.

It's November, and Lainey and I are walking home through the first snowstorm of the year. Chris has detention—he got caught listening to his iPod in class—and Em stayed to study with Sarah in the library until he can leave. Lainey and I started out holding hands when we left the school yard, but for the past two blocks, she's been chasing the big fat snowflakes, trying to catch them on her tongue.

"I *love* winter!" she tells me.

She twirls around with her arms outspread. Passersby smile at her antics. In the city, they'd probably think she was high on drugs. Here, they just put it down to teenage enthusiasm, which is exactly what it is. It's not that there aren't kids doing drugs in the Point. They're just not particularly obvious about it.

211

"Just wait until February," I say, "when you'll kill for some sunshine and a warm day."

"But you have seasons. How can you not love having seasons? Back home we had wet and dry, and we never had snow."

"I'm not saying I hate winter," I say.

"But you just don't love, love, love it!" she sings as she skips around me.

I have to admit that her happiness is contagious.

"Maybe I could learn to," I tell her.

She smiles and joins me again, slipping her hand under my arm.

"I like a bloke who's willing to learn," she says, and leans her head against my shoulder.

We continue like that, strolling arm in arm, the snow falling around us. It's like we're walking through some old postcard of a winter wonderland. I know. Can I be more mushy? But it's moments like this that you want to hold on to forever—you never want them to end.

"Johnny came by last night," she says after a while. "He and Em must have stood on the back porch for hours, just talking and talking."

"And?" I ask when she doesn't go on.

She shrugs. "I'm not really sure. She says they won't be getting back together, but then Johnny told her that didn't matter, because, even if they never saw each other again, they were still betrothed."

"He really used that word?"

She punches me in the arm. "Shut up, you. And he did."

"Sounds a little stalkerish to me."

"Well, I think it was romantic, and I think Em did, too. Did you notice that she seemed more cheerful today?"

"Now that you mention it, she wasn't scowling all the time, was she?"

That got me another light punch on the arm.

"Joking," I say.

She knows that I went and talked to Johnny, and, considering the history he and I have, it totally impressed her. Impressing her wasn't the reason I did it—we both know that—but it's always nice to look good to your girlfriend.

"Do you think we'll be together forever?" she asks as we come up on Lighthouse Street.

I smile, because it's a question I've been wondering myself, but I didn't have the courage to ask.

"I don't know," I tell her, "but I hope so."

She snuggles closer to me. "Me, too," she says.

Moments.

I don't want this one to end, either.

Charles de Lint is widely credited with having pioneered the contemporary fantasy genre with his urban fantasy *Moonheart* (1984). He has been a seventeen-time finalist for the World Fantasy Award, winning in 2000 for his short-story collection *Moonlight and Vines*; its stories are set in de Lint's popular fictional city of Newford, as are his novels *Little (Grrl) Lost, The Blue Girl,* and selected stories in the collection *Waifs and Strays* (a World Fantasy Award Finalist).

He has received glowing reviews and numerous other awards for his work, including the singular honor of having eight books chosen for the reader-selected Modern Library "Top 100 Books of the Twentieth Century."

A professional musician for more than twenty-five years, specializing in traditional and contemporary Celtic and American roots music, he frequently performs with his wife, MaryAnn Harris—fellow musician, artist, and kindred spirit.

Charles de Lint and MaryAnn Harris live in Ottawa, Ontario, Canada, and their respective Web sites are www.charlesdelint.com and www.reclectica.com.